Praise for KJ Charles
The Magpie Lord

"This combination of magic, mystery, and mayhem will have crossover appeal for fans of several genres; an exciting new voice in the paranormal world."

~ *Library Journal*

"Sexual tension between the two men is sizzling, yet subordinate to Charles's clever dialogue and imaginatively creepy magic."

~ *Publishers Weekly*

"This book was a wonderful surprise. I had never heard of this writer before, but I will certainly be on the lookout for more books from her."

~ *Dear Author*

"The story is funny and engaging. [...] Both MCs were three dimensional characters and likeable without being perfect or bland."

~ *Reviews by Jessewave*

"Anyone who's looking for something new and different with a historical flavor should pick up *The Magpie Lord*. It's a truly unique book, and I can't wait for the next entry in the series."

~ *Joyfully Reviewed*

Look for these titles by
KJ Charles

Now Available:

Non-Stop Till Tokyo
Think of England

A Charm of Magpies
The Magpie Lord
A Case of Possession

The Magpie Lord

KJ Charles

SAMHAIN
PUBLISHING

Samhain Publishing, Ltd.
11821 Mason Montgomery Road, 4B
Cincinnati, OH 45249
www.samhainpublishing.com

The Magpie Lord
Copyright © 2013 by KJ Charles
Print ISBN: 978-1-61922-114-7
Digital ISBN: 978-1-61921-576-4

Editing by Anne Scott
Cover by Lou Harper

First Samhain Publishing, Ltd. electronic publication: September 2013
First Samhain Publishing, Ltd. print publication: September 2014

Dedication

For Charlie, of course

One for sorrow
Two for joy
Three for a girl
Four for a boy
Five for silver
Six for gold
Seven for a secret never to be told
Eight for a letter over the sea
Nine for a lover as true as can be

One for sorrow
Two for mirth
Three for a funeral
Four for a birth
Five for heaven
Six for hell
Seven's the Devil his own self

Chapter One

The grey awful misery tangled round his heart and throat, choking him, sickening him with the vileness of his own nature. The shame and self-loathing too deep for repentance, too deep for words. Too deep for anything but the knife and the red flow and the longed-for emptiness of the end...

The voice seemed to come from a long distance away. "My lord? My lord! Oh, Jesus. My lord! You stupid sod!"

A slap, hard, round his face. He registered it through the haze of grey misery, then felt strong hands dragging him onto his feet and out of the room. His wrist hurt. He needed to finish the job.

He lunged clumsily back towards the knife, only to find his arm twisted up behind his back and a hard tug pulling him off balance.

"Out. This way." He was marched forward, pushed, dragged, the litany of doom pounding in his mind. All he could think of was ending it, making the unbearable guilt and shame stop, removing the foul stain of his soul from the world...

He vaguely noticed the hard grip on the back of his head, just before his face was plunged into icy, greasy water and held there, ruthlessly hard, as he inhaled a lungful of dirty dishwater, and something around his mind snapped.

KJ Charles

Lord Crane jerked his head out of the suddenly relaxed grip, came up spluttering but entirely alert, gasped for air, and kicked backwards viciously, aiming to cripple his attacker with a rake of his foot across the kneecap. The grizzled man in black had already jumped out of the way, though, and was standing back, holding up his hands in a gesture of nonaggression that Crane had no intention of testing.

Crane held himself ready to fight for a second, registered that he had just been half-drowned in the butler's sink by his manservant, let out a long breath and dropped his shoulders.

"It happened again," he said.

"Yes."

"*Tsaena.*" He shook his head, sending grey water flying from his hair, and blinked the liquid out of his eyes.

Merrick threw him a dishtowel. He caught it in his left hand, sucked in a hiss at the pain as his wrist moved, and mopped his face. He spat in the sink to get the taste of foul water and bitter leaves out of his mouth. "Son of a bitch. It happened again."

"Yes," said Merrick, with some restraint. "I *know*. I found you sawing at your wrist with a fucking table knife, my lord, which was what gave me the clue."

"Yes, alright." Crane pulled over a chair with a screech of wood on tile. "Can you...?" He gestured at his left wrist. The shirt cuff was unfastened and rolled back. He didn't remember doing that. He didn't remember the other times.

Merrick was already setting out lint and a roll of bandages, as well as a bottle of volatile-smelling spirit.

"I'll have some if you're pouring. *Ow.*"

"I reckon that's enough killing yourself for one evening." Merrick dabbed the raw wound with the raw alcohol. "Jesus,

10

this is deep, you'd have done yourself for sure with anything sharper. My lord—"

"*I don't know.* I was reading a book, thinking about getting dressed. I didn't..." He waved his right hand vaguely, and slapped it down on the worn tabletop. "God damn it."

There was silence in the kitchen. Merrick wound bandage carefully round the bloody wrist. Crane leaned his right elbow on the table and propped his head on his hand.

"I don't know what to do."

Merrick gave him a steady look from under his thin brows, and returned to his work.

"I don't know," Crane repeated. "I can't—I don't think I can do this any more. I can't..." *I can't bear it.* He'd never said the words in thirty-seven years, not even in the times of hunger and degradation. He wanted to say them now.

Merrick frowned. "Got to fight it, my lord."

"Fight *what*? Give me something to fight, and I'll fight it— but how the hell do I fight my own mind?"

"It ain't your mind," said Merrick levelly. "You ain't mad."

"Right. I can see how you reached that conclusion." Crane made a sound that was a little, though not very much, like a laugh. "After all these years, after he's bloody dead, it looks like the old bastard is finally getting rid of me."

Merrick began rolling up the lint and bandages with care. "You're thinking about that word again."

"*Hereditary*," enunciated Crane, staring at his narrow-fingered hands. "Hereditary insanity. We might as well put the name to it, no?"

"No," said Merrick. "Cos, I'll tell you what word I'm thinking of."

Crane's brows drew together. "What?"

Merrick's hazel eyes met Crane's and held them. He put the bottle of spirits back down on the table with a deliberate clink. "Shaman."

There was a silence.

"We're not in Shanghai now," said Crane eventually.

"No, we ain't. But if we was there, and you started going mad all on a sudden and off again, you wouldn't be sat there whining, would you? You'd be right out—"

"To see Yu Len."

Merrick cocked his head in agreement.

"But we're not in Shanghai," Crane repeated. "This is London. Yu Len is half the world away, and at this rate I'm not going to make it to next quarter day."

"So we find a shaman here," said Merrick simply.

"But—"

"No buts!" The words rang off the stone floor and tiled walls. "You can go to some mad-doctor and get thrown in the bedlam, or you can sit there and go mad for thinking you're going mad, or we find a fucking shaman and get this looked at like we would back home, because hereditary my *arse*." Merrick leaned forward, hands on the table, glaring in his master. "I know you, Lucien Vaudrey. I seen you look death in the face plenty of times, and every time you either ran like hell or you kicked him in the balls, so don't you tell me you want to die. I never met anyone who didn't want to die as much as you don't. So we are going to find a shaman and get this sorted, unless you got any better ideas, which you don't! *Right?*"

Merrick held his gaze for a few seconds, then straightened and began to tidy up. Crane cleared his throat. "Are there English shamans?"

"Got to be, right? Witches. Whatever."

"I suppose so," said Crane, trying hard, knowing it was pointless, knowing he owed it to Merrick. "I suppose so. Who'd know..." His fingers twitched, calling up memories. "Rackham. He's back, isn't he? I could ask him."

"Mr. Rackham," agreed Merrick. "We'll go see him. Ask for a shaman. You got any idea where he is?"

"No." Crane flexed his bandaged wrist and rose. "But if I can't find him through any of the clubs, we can just hang around all the filthiest opium dens in Limehouse till we meet him."

"See?" said Merrick. "Things are looking up already."

Chapter Two

Crane checked the carriage clock in his drawing room again. Apparently time was standing still; certainly the hands had not moved perceptibly since he last looked.

"Have a drink," recommended Merrick, who was finding minor tasks around the room. Crane didn't know if he was keeping an eye out for suicide attempts or just equally nervous about the arrival of the promised shaman.

"You have a damn drink, this is your fault," he said unfairly. "God knows what this character will be like." *It won't work. You're going to die. You deserve it.*

"What do you call an English shaman then?" asked Merrick. "Did Mr. Rackham say?"

"We were speaking Shanghainese. I've no idea. Warlock, probably, or something equally ridiculous."

"But Mr. Rackham—"

"Yes, yes. He said he was real, he said he was good, he said he would come at half past seven. I don't have anything else to tell you, so stop asking." *Brute. Ingrate. You ruined his life too.*

"Twitchy, aren't you?" Merrick observed. "My lord."

"Oh, shut up."

Crane stalked round the room, too on edge to sit. He had always found hope harder to deal with than despair. Despair didn't get disappointed. And if you hoped, you were always a suppliant, begging for crumbs, and Crane did not take pleasure in supplication. Quite the reverse.

But somewhere in the roiling misery a thread of hope refused to die. If this was truly an English shaman... If this was a shaman problem, not his father's blood legacy... If his mind was still his own...

The doorbell rang. Merrick almost ran to answer it. Crane very carefully didn't follow. He stood in the drawing room, hearing the exchange in the hall—"Mr. Rackham asked me to call. I'm here to see Lucien Vaudrey,"—and waited for the door to open.

"Your visitor, sir." Merrick ushered the shaman in.

He was incredibly unimpressive. Short, for one thing, barely five feet tall, narrow shouldered, significantly underweight, hollow-cheeked. He had reddish-brown hair cut unfashionably close, possibly against a hint of curls. His worn suit of faded black was obviously cheap and didn't fit terribly well; bizarrely, he wore cheap cotton gloves. He looked like a clerk, the ten-a-penny kind who drudged in every counting house, except that he had tawny-gold eyes that were vividly glowing in his pale rigid face, and they were staring at Crane with something that looked extraordinarily like hate.

"I'm Lucien Vaudrey," said Crane, extending his hand.

"You're Lord Crane," said the visitor, not extending his. "I had to be sure. But you're a Vaudrey of Lychdale, aren't you?"

Crane looked at the naked hostility in the other man's face and posture, and strolled to a conclusion, since it hardly required him to jump.

"I take it you've encountered my brother, Hector," he said. "Or possibly my father."

"Both." The little man spat the word out. "Oh, I've encountered your family alright. It's something of an irony to be sent to help one of you."

Crane shut his eyes for a second. *To hell with you, Father, if you're not already there. You won't rest till you've destroyed me, will you?* He struggled to control his voice against the anger, the crushing despair. "And your purpose in coming here tonight is to tell me that any member of my family can go to the devil? Very well. Consider me told, and be damned to you."

"Sadly, I don't have that luxury," said the visitor, upper lip curling into what was meant as a sneer but ended up a snarl. "Your friend Mr. Rackham demanded a favour on your behalf."

"Not a terribly impressive favour," said Crane, his own sneer calling on eight generations of earldom, as well as the gaping hole in his chest where hope had been. They had waited four days for this man during which he had had another attack. Everything had depended on this last throw of the dice. "I understood he was sending a shaman, not a pint-sized counter-jumper."

The other man dumped his battered carpetbag on the floor and clenched his fists. He took a belligerent stride forward, aggressively close to Crane, so that he was staring up into the much taller man's face. "My name is Stephen Day." He jabbed a finger into Crane's chest. "And—"

He stopped there, mouth slightly open. Crane very deliberately pushed his hand away. Day didn't react, the hand held in midair. Crane raised an eyebrow. "And?"

Day's reddish brows twitched, drew together. His tawny eyes were staring into Crane's, but not quite focusing, his pupils wide and black. He tilted his head to one side, then the other.

"*And?* Did you by any chance meet Mr. Rackham in an opium hell?" enquired Crane coldly.

"Yes," Day said. "Give me your hand."

"What?"

Day grabbed Crane's hand with both his gloved hands and stared at it. Crane pulled back angrily. Day kept his left-hand grip, but raised his right hand to his mouth, and dragged his glove off with his teeth. He spat it onto the floor, and said, "This will feel strange," as he seized Crane's hand with his bare skin.

"Christ!" yelped Crane, trying again to pull away, this time with alarm. Day's grip tightened. Crane looked down with disbelief. Aside from a jagged scar running across his left knuckles, Day's hands looked perfectly normal, if rather large for his small frame. Lightly dusted with dark hairs, gripping and turning Crane's fingers, but everywhere Day's skin touched his, he could feel a tingling flow, like a thousand tiny cold pinpricks, alive, electric, streaming into his blood. He gritted his teeth. Day's thumb gently brushed over the inside of his wrist, and he felt the skin rise into goose pimples.

"What the *hell* is that?"

"Me." Day released Crane's hand long enough to remove his second glove, also with his teeth, then grabbed it again. "Well, someone wants you dead. How long has this been going on?"

"About two months." Crane didn't bother to question what the man meant. The fizzing sensation was getting stronger, rising through his fingers into his wrists, prickling at the wound under the bandage.

"Two *months?* How many times have you attempted suicide?"

"Four," said Crane. "Three times in the last fortnight. I think I'm going to succeed soon."

"I'm amazed you've failed to date." Day scowled. "Alright. I am going to deal with it, because I owe Mr. Rackham a favour, and because this is not something that should happen to anyone, even a Vaudrey. My fee is ten guineas—for you, twenty. Don't argue it, because I would measure your remaining lifespan in hours rather than days right now. Don't provoke me, because I will not need much provocation to walk away. You'll need to answer my questions fully and frankly, and do what I tell you. Is that clear?"

Crane looked at the other man's intent face. "Can you stop what's happening to me?"

"I wouldn't be here otherwise."

"Then I accept your terms. Are you really a shaman?" The pulsing counsel of grey despair was beating at his mind, a large part of him wanted to kick the little swine downstairs, and the smaller man's roiling anger did not inspire confidence in his goodwill, but Crane's hand was electric with the current flowing through Day's fingers, and those tawny irises were almost completely obliterated by huge black pupils. Crane had seen Yu Len's eyes dilated in the same way, and a tendril of genuine, terrified hope was unfurling once more through the darkness.

"I don't know what a shaman is." Day looked Crane up and down, head slightly cocked, squinting. "Sit, and tell me about it."

Crane sat. Day pulled up a footstool and knelt on it, looking intently at—through?—Crane's head.

"I came back to England four months ago, after my father's death," Crane began.

Day's eyes met his for a second. "Your father died two years ago."

"Yes. I came back here four months ago. Spent the first couple of months ploughing through the mess my father made of his affairs. No problems." He refrained with an effort from jerking his head back as Day put a hand up next to his face, fingers moving oddly. "I went down to Piper two months ago when I could no longer put it off. You're acquainted with my family, do you know the house?"

"Not to visit." Day's gaze and tone were remote, and his fingers were twitching the air around Crane's face, picking and flicking at nothing.

"Well. I was in the library at Piper, working on the account books, and I was overcome by this appalling sense of misery and shame and self-loathing. Horror. Despair. It was dreadful. But it stopped as abruptly as it started, and, since Piper is not a happy house, I put it down to a strange mood. And then the next night, I sat down with a whisky and a book, and the next thing I was fully aware of, Merrick, my man, was shouting at me because I'd tried to hang myself from the bell rope." His voice was tight and unemotional. "I have no memory of doing that, just of Merrick dragging me down."

Day's eyes flicked up to Crane's again. "Then?"

"I left," Crane said with a sardonic twist of the lips. "Ran away back to London. And—it's absurd, but I almost forgot about it. It seemed like something that happened to someone else. I was entirely myself again. Then I had to go back down to Piper a couple of weeks ago. The first two days were fine. But the next evening...same thing. I tried to cut my wrist that time."

"Where?"

Crane indicated the point on his wrist. Day exhaled through his nostrils. "Where in the *house*?"

"Oh. The library."

"Was the first time in the library as well?"

"Yes."

"Has anything happened outside that room?"

"Not in Piper. But after we got back, last week, it began to happen here. I tried to cut my wrist six days ago, and again last night."

"Location?"

"This room."

Day sat back on his heels. "Do you recall the times of the episodes?"

"The evening, always. Time tends to feel a little vague."

"Mmm. Now, I need you to think carefully about this. Have you, since your return from China, ever spent an evening in the library at Piper *without* one of these attacks?"

Crane considered. "I don't think so," he said finally.

"And before the first attack here, had you spent an evening in this room without an attack?"

"Yes, several."

"And, after these episodes, did your mouth taste of ivy?"

Crane felt a cold prickle run down his spine. "Yes," he said, as calmly as he could. "Or, at least, bitter green leaves. Strongly. And, ah...the very first time I felt it, the room smelled of the same thing. Stank of it."

"Yes, it would. What did you bring back from Piper?"

"Bring back?"

"An object. A box. Furniture. A coat with something in its pockets. Something came from the library at Piper on or after your last visit and it is here now. What is it?"

Crane looked blankly around the room. The mansion flat was a self-contained set of rooms in one of the new buildings on the Strand. He, or rather Merrick, had hung the walls with scrolls and paintings brought back from China. But he'd had no furniture and, although he hadn't been poor for years and was now very rich indeed, Piper was full of unused items, and careful habits were hard to break. The room was full of ancient dark wooden pieces, vaguely familiar, not worth noticing.

"Most of the furniture is from Piper," he said. "The chests, the table—"

"Since your last visit down?" Day interrupted.

"Some of it, I think. I'm not sure. I don't pay a lot of attention to these things. But I know a man who does. You might as well come in," Crane went on without raising his voice.

Merrick opened the door with some dignity. "My lord," he said. "We brought back a number of items on our most recent return, Mr. Day. That picture was, I believe, in the library at Piper." Day leapt up to inspect it, running his fingers over the frame, ignoring the image. "There were also a number of books, sir. They have been placed on these shelves."

"Together?" asked Day, staring at the crowded shelves that covered an entire wall.

"No, sir."

"Blast."

Day moved over to the shelf and spread his hands out over the spines of several books, fingers twitching slightly. "Nothing is leaping out at me. Lord Crane, I suggest you leave before it happens again and let me try to find it on my own."

"Find *what*? Do you know what's happening to me?"

"It's a Judas jack." Day turned a thick book over in his hands. "No question about that. We're looking for something about the size of an apple. Wooden. You brought something back with this thing in it, and it's in this room somewhere. Now, Mr. Merrick, please take Lord Crane out of this building, and keep him away for a couple of hours. He should not be here in the evening till I find this thing, and it's nearly eight already."

Crane and Merrick glanced automatically at the clock. Merrick said, hesitantly, "My lord, that ain't the library clock from Piper, is it?"

Crane's brows drew together. "It looks like it. Ugly thing. But you brought it, you should know."

"I didn't bring it. It turned up here. I thought you brought it."

"No," said Crane carefully. "No, I don't recall doing that."

Day looked at the carriage clock that stood on the mantelpiece. It showed one minute to eight. He flexed his hands before reaching out and picking it up.

"The back's locked," he observed. "It's big enough. And...a clock, and it happens at the same time... Lord Crane, leave. Get out. Mr. Merrick, get rid of him *now*."

"Yes, sir—oh shit," said Merrick as the clock began to strike and Crane took a horrible, sucking breath.

Chapter Three

The greyness came on Crane harder and faster than before. He could taste the ivy in his mouth now, feel the assault on his mind, almost hear, somewhere outside hearing, a whispering of voices.

damned

worthless

die

He wasn't aware he was going for a knife. He only vaguely heard Day bellow, "Hold him!" There was a pain, and for some reason his knees buckled, and some force was stopping him from getting the knife that meant sweet oblivion, release, the fresh flow of blood he owed. He thrashed and kicked, and heard the shouts and thumps as though they were happening a long way away, even the yell of alarm right in his ear, and suddenly the greyness receded, and he was face down on the drawing room rug, with both arms twisted behind his back and a heavy weight pinning him to the ground. The breathy flow of whispered Shanghainese obscenities identified his assailant as Merrick.

"I'm all right," he said, muffled. "I'm all right. Get off me, you lump."

"Don't," Day said from the end of the room. "Keep him down."

Crane angled his neck uncomfortably. Day was also on the floor, kneeling by the fireplace. His left hand was held rigid, just above the floor, its fingers contorted into splayed claws. Under it was something Crane couldn't quite see. Day had the abstracted look again, his lips were slightly drawn back from his teeth, and from where Crane lay, his eyes seemed to be pure darkness with a ring of white.

"Let me up," Crane snapped.

"Don't let him up," Day repeated. "Don't let him move. Break his arms if you have to."

"*Day—*"

"I'm having a certain amount of trouble holding this thing." Day's voice had a slight tremor of tension to it. "And I need it held, but the nodes... I'm making this too complicated. This is craft. Wood, blood and birdspit. Where's my bag?"

"By the door," said Merrick.

Day looked over at the bag, several feet away, and let out a hiss of annoyance. He sat back slightly, stretching out his right hand, and something leapt from the bag, hit the ground with a clang and a rattle, and rolled towards the clerk-like man, stopping within his reach.

"Oh my Gawd," said Merrick.

Day picked it up. It was a pack of metal knitting needles. He pulled one out with his mouth and discarded the pack, holding the long needle in his free hand. His face tightened, a man trying to work out an irritating puzzle.

He put the sharp end of the needle back between his lips, and pulled at the other end, and the metal stretched, elongating in sudden jerks, thinning like pulled toffee, twisting and writhing.

"*Tsaena*," hissed Merrick and Crane, simultaneously obscene.

Day kept working, face intent, his other hand steady in its clawed position over the floor. Finally he took the distorted needle out of his mouth. It was bizarrely corkscrewed, and obviously sharply pointed.

"That's iron," whispered Merrick.

Day wiped his mouth on the back of his hand. There was a faint smell of scorched metal in the air. "Tin," he said. "If I could do that with iron, it would be impressive. Right. I'm going to pull this thing's teeth. It isn't going to be pleasant." He shifted position, and suddenly the feelings were back, pounding into Crane's skull, waves of misery wracking his entire body. He wanted to curl up in a corner, howl, die.

"The thing is," said Day in a hatefully calm voice, "I need to bring it closer to you to see what I'm doing, and take off the hold I've got on it. And that's going to make it quite a lot worse. Can you bear it?"

Crane shut his eyes, bit at the carpet. No, he couldn't. It couldn't be worse. He would rather die than have it worse. He just wanted it all to be over.

"He can take it," said Merrick.

Day hesitated.

"I know what he can take." Merrick's tone brooked no argument. "Do it. Now. Sir."

"Get on with it, damn you," Crane added violently, because he had to force the words out through the overwhelming misery that clogged his throat.

"Very well. Mr. Merrick, are you capable of holding him down?"

"Yes."

25

"Good. Don't let him move." Day paused, and added stiffly, "You have my assurance that I will make this as quick as I can."

He moved awkwardly forward, without rising. He was, Crane saw, pushing the thing along the floor, but pushing apparently without touching it, his fingers still clawed above it.

It came closer, and the hairs were standing on Crane's arms. The air was feeling greasy and dry and dirty and foul, like a filthy old sheepskin. He tried to recoil, and was held down hard.

"Don't move, now," muttered Merrick.

Day had the thing in front of Crane's face.

It was gnarled wood, carved in a roughly humanoid shape, riddled with holes. It seemed to be pulsing slightly. It looked as though it would feel oily. It was on some indefinable level utterly obscene, and Crane was overwhelming, painfully frightened of it. He pulled his head back.

"Steady," whispered Merrick. "Come on, Vaudrey, you've done worse."

But he hadn't, nothing worse than this, because as Day moved his hand away, the malevolence of the thing poured out in a flood of foul cancerous air that flooded into Crane's nose and mouth and eyes. He knew he was screaming and thrashing, he could feel Merrick's grip putting pressure on his elbows and knees, but he couldn't bear it, couldn't stand another second. The malignancy was all-consuming, shrivelling his soul to a single point of unbearable pain, and he was fighting Merrick hard, and Day was simply sitting there, probing the device with the twisted needle. Crane cursed him, the fucking vicious ginger dwarf, what the hell had he ever done to him, and Merrick, whose fucking fault this was, and himself, in the foulest language at his command, crying, begging, until Day spoke, in a voice that he could hardly hear through the filthy miasma around him.

"This will hurt."

The agony came like a knife, pulsed through Crane's chest and back and arms and upper thighs like screaming burning fire...

And then it didn't.

Stephen sat back on his heels and wiped his forehead as Lord Crane slumped forward, boneless. The manservant Merrick straddled his back, white and sweating, blood drooling from his nose where Crane had landed a blow earlier. He glared down at his master and over at Stephen with a murderous look.

Stephen dropped the gnarled piece of wood to the ground and took a very deep breath.

"You can get off him. It's done."

"My lord?" said Merrick, releasing Crane's arms. "My lord?"

There was a sort of muffled sobbing from where Crane's face rested in the carpet. His body was shaking.

Merrick clambered off his back and peered down. "My lord? You all right?" He looked up at Stephen, eyes full of lethal promise. "What did you do to him?"

Crane made a grunting noise, lifted his head, pushed himself up onto his knees. There were tears in his eyes, and a huge grin on his face.

"Oh my God," he said. "Oh my God, it's gone. It's gone. Oh God, Merrick." He lunged forward and grabbed the startled manservant, hugging him hard. "You bloody genius, getting a shaman. Pulled my arse out of the fire, again. I love you. And you," he said to Stephen. "You're a god-damned magician. Well, exactly, that's what you *are*, a magician! Oh my God, a shaman, and it worked. It's *amazing*. Do you know, I never noticed what a beautiful room this is. Just look at that carpet! You need to see it close up to appreciate it, of course. Lie on it, that's the dandy."

"What's wrong with him?" demanded Merrick.

Stephen rose. He felt drained. "Nothing's wrong. It's just euphoria. He's been fighting that thing very hard for a long time, and he's gone the other way. He'll calm down."

Crane bounced to his feet, grabbed Stephen's hand, gave a startled jolt, and shook it vigorously. "You're *wonderful*. And your hands are wonderful. Merrick, you should try this, they're like...lots of little bubbles. Champagne! Hands like champagne! Do you know, Day, there's a house in Shanghai where they import champagne and what they do, they pour it over your—"

"The shaman does *not* want to hear about that," Merrick put in hastily. "Sir—"

"Fresh air," Stephen said firmly. "Is there a garden?"

They wrestled Crane's coat on and walked him down the back stairs, to avoid notice, and round to the private garden of the mansion block. It was a stunning April night, still warm, with a large yellow moon hanging over the London sky. There were a few shadowy figures moving around, fellow residents taking the air. Completely oblivious to them, Crane leapt onto a bench and began to declaim in what sounded to Stephen like Chinese.

"What's that?" he asked the manservant.

"Poem about the moon. He doesn't do poems till the third bottle, mostly. How long's this going to last, sir?"

"Not long," Stephen assured him. "It'll do him no harm. In fact, I imagine he's having a marvellous time. Is that still about the moon?" he added. He didn't understand a word, but Crane's tone transcended language.

"Not that bit, sir, no. Gawd, I hope nobody round here speaks Shanghainese. Oi, you, my lord, get down from there."

"Look at the lovely flowers, Lord Crane," Stephen suggested. Merrick gave him an incredulous look, but Crane leapt down from the bench and began to investigate the flowerbeds with enthusiasm. Magician and manservant fell into step behind him.

"I thought we were in trouble there," said Merrick. "You saved his life, sir."

"Probably." Stephen sounded no more enthusiastic than he felt. He jammed his hands in his pockets and hunched his shoulders. "Mr. Merrick...in what capacity do you serve Lord Crane? What do you actually do?"

"Manservant," said Merrick.

"Everything!" Crane span round, arms wide. "Factotum, man of all work, business partner, bodyguard. My second self. He speaks with my voice. Or do I speak with his voice? Which way round is it?"

"You speak a lot of rubbish," said Merrick. "Go on, look at the pretty flowers. Something to say, sir?"

Stephen rubbed his chin. "The Judas jack didn't happen by accident. Someone made that thing to kill. It's a murder weapon."

Merrick gave him a long, level look. "A shaman murderer. After his lordship."

"Yes."

"Going to have to do something about that, then."

"Yes. I need to think. And to talk to him when he's not so...exhilarated."

Crane looked round to see the two men staring at him. He flashed Merrick a gleeful grin. "Are you talking to the shaman?

Has he cheered up yet? If I had hands like that, I'd be cheerful *all the time*."

"I bet you bloody would," Merrick told him. "Shut up."

"You should smile more," Crane added to Stephen. "You'd be quite pretty if you weren't so miserable."

Merrick made a stifled noise and started talking in rapid Chinese.

Stephen propped his back against a tree trunk and flexed his hands, stretching the tendons, watching master and man. Crane, tall and lean, was standing on one leg, face alight with glee, pale blond hair shining silver in the moonlight. Merrick, shorter, grizzled and bright-eyed, was shaking his head but grinning.

Euphoria was like drunkenness in some ways. *In vino veritas*. Stephen had no idea what Crane was saying, but it didn't map onto how he imagined Hector Vaudrey in the grip of euphoria, if the man had been capable of it at all.

Stephen closed his eyes and cursed internally. It would be a great deal easier to walk away if Lucien Vaudrey was cast in the same mould as his brother Hector, and he wanted to walk away, very badly.

He needed to clear his mind. He listened to the Chinese syllables for a few moments more as he calmed his breathing, the distorted vowels sliding up and down the tonal scale in a deeply alien way. Then he stretched out his hands and let his fingers do the hearing.

The etheric flow rushed past, tingling through his nerve endings. Crane's effervescent, unnatural hilarity bubbled through the ether, whisking away the remnants of the jack's stain. Merrick was a solid presence, earth to Crane's air, blocking the flow. The tide was coming in up the Thames, not far away, and he sensed salt water rippling, the surge of boats, wet wood and sailcloth, the quiet throb of the garden around him, but mostly he could feel Crane, sharp and silver, standing out from the surrounding world like a knife in a drawer full of wooden spoons.

Champagne hands, he thought, as he fell into the ether.

"Mr. Day?"

Stephen blinked himself out of his reverie and glanced at the moon. He wasn't sure how long he had been there, pulling strength from the etheric flow that ran through him, but he felt rather better. There was a distinct chill in the night air, and Crane was looking at him, slightly puzzled, and definitely sober.

"Yes," he said. "I beg your pardon, I was thinking. How are you feeling, Lord Crane?"

"Normal. Not consumed by misery. Not going mad. My arms hurt like blazes, and I'm embarrassed to recall that I said a variety of offensive things to you, but otherwise I've never felt better. I've spent the last two months under a shadow, and I'm only realising how dark it was now it's lifted. I owe you a very great deal, Mr. Day. I understand your repugnance at my family name, but..."

He held out his hand. Stephen hesitated, but forced himself to take it. He watched Crane's face as bare skin touched and saw no repulsion there, just startled interest.

"That's still remarkable, even when I'm in my right mind. What *is* it?"

"Hard to explain." Stephen had no intention of explaining. "I work with my hands."

"It's...magic?"

"Could we go inside? If you're not too tired, there are some things I think we need to discuss."

Chapter Four

The Judas jack was lying on the floor where Stephen had dropped it. It looked like a piece of gnarled old wood, nothing more. Crane prodded it with the toe of his shoe.

"Don't touch it," Stephen told him. "I'll get rid of it."

"Thank you," said Crane. "You know, I feel in need of a drink. I don't suppose that would be acceptable?"

"Ah... Yes. Thank you."

Crane hesitated. "I've no idea what we have other than wine, whisky, brandy and port. Water?"

"Wine, thank you."

"You drink wine? Really?"

"Yes...why not?"

"Shamans don't," said Crane. "Yu Len would storm out of the room leaving curses in his wake if I defiled his spiritual purity with this particularly good Burgundy."

"I'm not a shaman." Stephen tasted the wine he was handed. "Fortunately." He didn't often drink good wine, but he had no trouble detecting the quality here.

"What are you, exactly?" Crane enquired.

"A practitioner."

"Practitioner. What does that mean?"

"It describes what I do, in a way that's meaningful to other people who do similar things," said Stephen. "There are other words with which you're doubtless more familiar."

"So I, as a layman, might call you a witch or a warlock?" suggested Crane, and immediately held his hands up in apology before Stephen could utter his angry response. "I beg your pardon if that was offensive, I really didn't mean to insult you."

Stephen took a calming breath. "A warlock is something else. I'm not a warlock."

"Noted." Crane sipped his wine. "Mr. Day, while you were, ah, thinking, Merrick told me what you said."

"Oh," said Stephen. "Yes."

"Is someone trying to kill me? By means of...practice?"

"Craft, actually, which is a slightly different thing. But yes. Someone set out to commit murder, and may try again."

"That's not a very inviting prospect."

"I don't suppose it is." Stephen produced a crumpled black and white feather from his pocket. "Tell me the significance of this."

"Where did that come from?"

"Out of the jack. Judas jacks work by a method called sympathy. Normally a jack might contain a lock of hair, nail clippings..."

"I think I know the principle," Crane said, somewhat to Stephen's surprise.

"Really? Well, yours had a magpie feather."

Crane shrugged. "It's the family badge. There are magpies carved all over the house, magpies in the family portraits, that sort of thing. My father's—my—signet ring. The grounds of Piper are infested with the things. Come to that, *piper* is a country word for magpie. It's very much a family symbol."

Stephen had been afraid he'd say that. "No intense personal significance to you?"

"Nothing I can think of. Apart from the tattoos, I suppose."

"You have tattoos?" Stephen had little direct experience of the nobility, but he was fairly sure they weren't meant to be inked like common sailors. Then again, they weren't supposed to swear like common sailors either. Lord Crane was definitely not meeting his expectations of aristocracy, or of the Vaudreys, come to that.

"I do." Crane's tone was unapologetic.

"Of magpies? May I see?"

Crane paused for a second. Then, moving deliberately, he undid his cufflinks and tossed them onto a side table, so that the gold clinked. He unbuttoned his shirt unhurriedly and shrugged it off in one fluent movement.

"Good Lord," said Stephen.

Black, white and blue, three magpies perched and cawed and flew over Crane's torso, the colours magnificently vibrant. Another bird stretched its wings on his left shoulder. He turned, and Stephen gave a tiny gasp as he saw the huge single magpie that brooded on his back, claws clutching a branch that was made of an old, jagged scar.

"Good *Lord*. What's that, five of them?"

"Seven."

Stephen peered round him, frowning slightly. "I only see five."

"The other two are lower down," said Crane. "Two for joy."

There was a blank moment before Stephen felt his face flood with scarlet, reddening further as he saw Crane's slight, untrustworthy grin.

"I see." He kept his voice determinedly neutral. "Is there a reason you have seven magpies tattooed on you?"

"Seven for a secret never to be told." Crane shrugged, making a magpie ripple. "Actually, I just ran out of useful space."

"Why any magpies at all?"

"Whim. I was being forced to have a very large and expensive tattoo, and it seemed a change from the usual dragons and carp. I rather liked it, as it turned out, so I added more."

"...forced to have a tattoo?"

"It's a long story."

Stephen couldn't tear his eyes away. Crane's body art was spectacular, but what it covered was equally striking: a muscular torso, powerful and much broader than he'd realised. Crane's height and the elegant tailoring made him look deceptively lean to a casual glance, but bare-chested, tattooed and scarred, this was unmistakably the hard body of a hard man. Stephen felt himself shiver suddenly.

He needed to look away now.

He turned abruptly, unable to do it with grace. Crane, apparently unembarrassed, reached out a long arm for his shirt and began to dress as Stephen pulled himself together.

"Right. Well, that might do it, but... You came back to England four months ago, yes? No visits before then?"

"None. I hadn't planned to return at all. Wouldn't have, but the lawyers were making a fuss."

"Mmm. Tell me how your father and brother died."

"Is that relevant?"

"I hope not."

Crane gave him a narrow-eyed look as he buttoned his shirt. "I'm told they both killed themselves. Hector hanged himself from the same bell rope I tried to use. Father shot himself."

"Where?"

"In the head." Stephen made an exasperated noise, and Crane gave a twitch of a smile. "Piper. In the library."

"Blast. Can we sit down? Lord Crane, the Judas jack was created to drive its victims to madness and self-murder. Its choice of victims was driven by the magpie feather, your family symbol. It was hidden in your family home. It would have been made to order, carved for its purpose, and that wood is clearly more than a few months old. It was in the Piper library until it came back here with you. So—"

"That device attacked my father and brother?" Crane's eyes were steady on Stephen's. "That's why they killed themselves? They experienced what I did?"

"Yes. I think so. It's *possible* that their suicides were coincidence, but the balance of likelihood is against that."

Crane nodded. He walked to the door, opened it, and bellowed, "Merrick!"

The manservant appeared almost before Lord Crane was seated again, and took a chair at his jerked thumb.

"The shaman thinks the jack thing got the old man and Hector," said Crane without preamble. "It was aimed at the family. A device to kill Vaudreys."

Merrick considered this, nodded slowly.

"Which raises a question," Crane went on. "Is someone trying to wipe out my entire family, or was it a trap for Hector and my father, and I fell into it?"

"That's a good question." Stephen looked at the aristocratic, emotionless face opposite him. "You don't seem surprised to learn your family may have been murdered."

Crane shrugged. "I always found it deeply improbable either of them killed himself. Hector was incapable of remorse, and it's much more plausible that my father was driven to suicide by sorcery than that he chose to clear my way to the succession. What seems to me very likely indeed is that someone hated them enough to kill them. And I find it very unlikely that person was trying to kill *me* because I haven't been here, so do we in fact have a problem?"

"Murder?" Stephen knew he sounded scathing, couldn't help it. "It is a crime."

"Mr. Day, you know what they were," Crane said. "If someone killed them, it was about bloody time."

"No, it was murder," said Stephen. "No matter what they were."

"I dispute that. Hector did exactly as he chose—rape, assault, abuse—with my father's protection and complicity, and he got away with it for thirty years and more because not one single person had the guts to stand up to them—"

"My father did."

Stephen was on his feet, he wasn't sure how, and his hand was clenched painfully round the sharp-edged crystal stem of his glass. Crane's eyes were on his, intent.

"Did he," he said calmly. "I didn't know that. Who is your father?"

"His name was Allan Day. Of Ruggleford."

"I don't know the name. When was this?"

"Sixteen years ago."

"After I'd left. He must have been a brave man," said Crane. "I take it things did not end well for him."

"Your father destroyed him." Stephen's throat was tight on the words. "His business, his reputation. His career. My mother. He brought an action—he was a solicitor—against your father's abuse of his position, for the sake of all the people who needed someone to stand up for them, and Hector Vaudrey—he threatened my mother, and when Father wouldn't back down—he came to our house—" The wine was slopping over the sides of the glass as his hand shook. "And, after, when Father gave in, they made him sign papers, admissions, of theft and malpractice. Lies. They humiliated him in court, then wherever we went after that, your father's lawyers made sure the lies were spread about him. If anyone hired him, there would be a letter sooner or later, and he'd be dismissed. Even when he was doing the most menial work, till we were reduced to nothing. There was no money to treat Mother when she fell ill, and—" He swallowed hard, staring with hatred at the arrogant, expressionless Vaudrey features before him. "My father died of a broken heart. Your father broke him."

He stopped, too raw to say anything else, waiting to see what defence the man would offer. The silence stretched.

"I can't apologise," said Crane, at last. "It wouldn't mean anything. Your father was a brave man who tried to do what was right, and mine was a callous, deluded fool who cared about nothing but that repulsive madman Hector."

Stephen groped for a response. He had expected dismissiveness, denial, something he could fight. He didn't know what to do with agreement.

"The fact that you came here at all, let alone saved my life, suggests that you take after your father," Crane went on. "I'd like you to believe that I don't entirely take after mine."

"I wasn't going to help you," Stephen jerked out. "I was going to tell you to go to hell. I couldn't even do that." He sat down abruptly and put his hand over his face.

"Here." Crane leaned forward with the bottle. Stephen's hand, holding his glass, was still shaking. Crane's fingers closed firmly round Stephen's wrist, holding the hand and glass steady as he poured, keeping the grip for a couple of seconds afterwards, calming, until Stephen took a deep breath and pulled away.

"One question." Crane settled back into his chair. "You mentioned my father's lawyers. Did you mean Griffin and Welsh?"

"Yes."

Crane nodded. "Mr. Day, I understand entirely why you don't want to be here and I don't blame you. I would appreciate it if you could tell me what now needs to happen, though."

Stephen took refuge in professional thought. "You need a practitioner to go down to Piper and confirm whether the jack was used to murder your father and brother. He needs to identify the maker, ascertain their motive, bring them to justice."

"Justice?"

"What was done to you is a crime. And if the jack was used on your family, they were murdered. Justice."

Crane exchanged glances with Merrick. "How exactly would one go about dealing with murder by magic? It would hardly be something to take to a judge and jury."

"Wrong." Stephen suddenly felt very tired. "There'll be a judge and jury. Of its kind."

Crane nodded. "Very well. Then the question is, are you able to recommend someone, a practitioner, to undertake this?"

Stephen's eyes flew to his face. Crane gave him a faintly sardonic look. "Please, Mr. Day, I'm not going to ask you to hunt down my father and Hector's killer. If you can recommend someone I'd be very grateful. If you can't, I'll go back to Rackham, and let him know his favour was well repaid."

"I'll find you someone," Stephen said. "I'm better placed to do that. They'll be in touch."

"Thank you. Let Merrick have your address. I doubt I'll see you again, Mr. Day, so accept my thanks. And for what it's worth, I'm sorry about your father."

"Thank you." Stephen managed a half smile. "I'm sorry about yours."

Crane tipped his glass in salute. "Yes. Aren't we all."

Chapter Five

It was the following Thursday, and hot. The iron girders that roofed Paddington Station shimmered in the heat that rose from the engines and beat down from the cloudless sky, more like August than April. Clouds of steam belched and rolled across the platforms. Metal screeched, porters bellowed, horns blared, and Stephen Day sprinted down a platform, dodging crowds of full-skirted ladies and the importunities of railway officials.

"Mr. Day!" yelled Merrick from the first-class carriages, waving, and Stephen ducked under a protesting guard's arm, threw his bag into the carriage, and made it onto the train a full four seconds before the wheels began to turn.

He slammed the door and collapsed onto a seat, trying not to suck in breath too noisily.

"You cut that fine," remarked Crane. "This is a surprise, I must say." He was wearing a superbly cut light-grey suit that matched the grey of his eyes, and looked cool and patrician and unruffled, as befitted a man who owned a sizeable part of Gloucestershire and could afford people to carry his bags. Stephen had run from Baker Street and could feel his face glowing and sweat running down his spine.

"I got held up." He was horribly uncomfortable, and he was not going to stand on ceremony. "Is there nobody else in here?"

"As you see."

"Then if you don't mind…"

Crane inclined his head. Stephen stripped off his gloves and his shabby coat with relief, grateful that no ladies were present. He slung his bag onto a luggage rack and sank back into a well-upholstered seat.

On the other row of seats, Merrick and Crane looked at him, and at each other.

"Busy morning, was it?" said Crane eventually. "Or a long night?"

"The latter, running into the former. Some business to take care of."

"So I see. Merrick, get a pot of coffee lined up for Mr. Day, strong, and on your way, tell the guard we're reserving this whole carriage to the end of the line. Encourage him not to come in. Get the blinds on your way out."

"My lord," said Merrick woodenly, pulling the blinds on the compartment door and letting himself out.

"Is there a reason you're making this a private compartment?" Stephen enquired warily.

"Yes," said Crane. "Is there a reason your sleeve is soaked in blood?"

"What? Where? Oh *bother*." Stephen contorted himself to look at his left elbow. "Blast."

"It looks to the untutored eye as though you have been leaning in a puddle of blood," said Crane. "Quite a large puddle."

"Yes. I dare say it does."

"Because…?"

"I can't talk about my business. I'm sure you understand."

"But since you're now about *my* business, Mr. Day, I'd like to know whose blood you're wearing. Within the bounds of discretion. For my own peace of mind."

Stephen gave him a narrow-eyed look. "It was a cat," he said. "And bleeding it wasn't my idea, I can assure you." He stifled a yawn.

There was a subdued knock and Merrick entered bearing a tray.

"Another small miracle, thank you." Crane nodded towards Stephen. "It's cat's blood, in case you were wondering."

"Course it is, my lord." Merrick manipulated cups and coffeepot deftly. "There you are, sir, that'll set you up. You won't be disturbed, my lord. Do you need me?"

"No, carry on," said Crane. Merrick said something in Chinese and there was a brief staccato exchange before Merrick withdrew again.

Stephen sipped his coffee, watching Crane over the cup's brim. "What was that?"

"I reminded him not to fleece the fireman too badly. He's a devil with a pack of cards. Why are you here, Mr. Day? We were expecting Mr. Fairley."

"Yes, I know. I, ah...I got your lawyer's letter."

The stiff cream vellum envelope, wildly incongruous as it lay on his doormat with the cheap stationery and the bills. The letter it contained, from Crane's lawyers, who were not Griffin and Welsh. The written, notarised statement from Humphrey Griffin, stating how he had forced Allan Day to sign the documents that had ruined him, laying out the lies, detailing the persecution he had subjected him to, all on the orders of Quentin, Lord Crane. The list of names to whom copies of that notarised statement were being sent, on the orders of Lucien, Lord Crane. The dry request that Stephen should supply names and addresses of any parties to whom further copies should be sent.

He had opened an envelope and found in it his father's long-lost reputation. And he had cried, then, kneeling in the hallway, for the first time in years.

"How did you get Griffin to admit all that, Lord Crane?" he asked now, leaning forward. "It's an admission of perjury as well as utterly disgraceful conduct. Why did he agree to write it?"

"I am in the process of nailing Mr. Humphrey Griffin to the wall so thoroughly that future generations will mistake him for a tapestry," said Crane. "Currently, he is under the impression that his cooperation may incline me not to press for a lengthy prison sentence for embezzlement, malpractice, extortion and perjury."

"Will it?"

Crane smiled, not pleasantly. "No. But it scarcely matters. When I have finished with him, Mr. Griffin will be begging for an extra ten years in gaol, just to have walls between himself and me."

"Oh," said Stephen. "Good."

Crane frowned. "I hope you're not here because of that. You owe me nothing."

"No. I know."

"So I ask again, Mr. Day, why are you here?"

"I'm here because I should be," Stephen said. "It was rather childish of me to walk away in the first place. I dealt with the jack, so I have a feeling for the maker, and I know the Lychdale area. It's obvious I should handle this."

Crane was looking at him with a raised brow. "It must have become obvious fairly recently, since Mr. Fairley introduced himself as your replacement yesterday."

"Ah." Stephen cursed internally. "You met him."

"I did, yes. I can't honestly say he inspired me with confidence in the matter of murder, although I'm sure that if I wanted a practitioner that I could take to all the best society parties and be sure of his many close acquaintances..."

Stephen shut his eyes. "Yes, he does, um, feel the importance of birth and breeding quite strongly."

"Frankly, I thought he was an oleaginous prick. I assume he has hidden talents."

"I'm sure he does," Stephen said, without conviction.

Even after the miraculous letter had arrived, he had not wanted to do this. If Hector and Quentin Vaudrey had been murdered, they should have justice, but it could be at someone else's hands. Then he had learned that the hands would be Fairley's, a soft self-indulgent parlour magician whose only qualification was his social connection, and Stephen's vow had stuck in his throat like a mouthful of brambles.

It had nothing to do with the mental image of Crane's long-fingered hands and lean, muscular, tattooed body, or the laugh lines around those lazy, perceptive grey eyes. Those irritatingly persistent memories gave him the strongest possible reason to stay away. No, it was as simple as it always was: justice had to be done. And since he had no authority to select the practitioner to do it, he had to do the job himself or stay out of the whole business.

Crane was looking at him curiously. "So why did you send that obsequious twit in the first place?"

"I didn't," said Stephen, slightly too honestly. "He, ah, he proposed himself. Feeling an earl would require a practitioner of birth and breeding." Stephen's talents outstripped Fairley's to an almost embarrassing degree, but he was the son of a provincial nobody who had died destitute; Fairley was the son of a baronet. Taking the job back had led to a heated exchange. He quoted, woodenly, "Nobility has a certain *je ne sais quoi* that demands the presence of a gentleman, not a hireling."

The eighth Earl Crane lifted an aristocratic brow. "In my case, the *je ne sais quoi* includes four years as a smuggler, two death sentences, and a decade as a Shanghai Joe, a dockfront trader. I hope you feel suitably elevated."

Stephen tried to confront all of this at once. "Two death sentences? Really? I mean, you look very well, considering."

Crane grinned at him. "One was in absentia. One wasn't, and I spent three days in a condemned cell. I can't recommend the experience."

"And—did you say a *smuggler*?"

"That was what the death sentences were for."

"What did you smuggle?" Stephen demanded, then caught himself. "Sorry, it's none of my business."

"Not at all," Crane said politely. "Silks and tea, mostly. Medicines, on occasion. And we ran the guns for an uprising against a particularly noxious tax farmer, but that was a favour to a friend, really."

"That's very..." Stephen couldn't think what it was. It occurred to him that if the man didn't wear such staggeringly expensive suits, the tanned, mocking face and tattoos would make him look exactly like someone's overheated fantasy of a smuggler in the exotic East. "Did your father know?"

"No idea." Crane didn't sound concerned. "He put me on a boat to China when I was seventeen, expressing the hope I'd die out there, and that was the last I ever heard from him. We didn't get on, you know."

"Yes," said Stephen. "I heard."

Crane shrugged. "He always disliked me, and I gave him plenty to dislike. He sent me off with no post, no acquaintances, no Chinese and no money, and I would undoubtedly have been dead within a year without Merrick, but as it happened, nothing could have suited me so well as Shanghai. It was five thousand miles away from Hector. So to answer your question as far as possible, I lived under my own name in China, I didn't do so with any subtlety, and while I never communicated with him again, someone else doubtless did. In all honesty, I stopped caring a very long time ago."

"I'm sorry," Stephen said involuntarily.

"What for?"

That your father was a swine. That my father's dead. That you're a Vaudrey. He grabbed for something that didn't sound like pity. "I made the assumption you were like him. Them. That was unfair."

"Understandable. A lot of people down in Lychdale make that assumption. Including, presumably, the jack's maker."

"We'll see about that."

"Indeed. And I remain of the opinion that if this maker did remove my brother from the world, I'd rather shake his hand than press charges."

"You might feel that," Stephen said. "And if he had shot him, I might agree with you. But if it was the jack, your brother and father were tortured to death, slowly, over months. And that kind of cruelty tends to be...habit-forming."

Crane's eyebrows shot up. "You think the maker does this sort of thing regularly?"

Stephen chose his words carefully. "They did a very cruel thing very competently, which suggests that they may have

48

done such things before, or that they may find it easy to do such things again. In any case, it is not acceptable to continue down this path unchecked."

"I see. Well, you're the expert. I'll leave it to your judgement."

Stephen gave a tired half smile. "Yes. People generally do."

It was a slow train and a hot day, and Day fell asleep well before they reached Lychdale. Merrick returned to find his master contemplating the unconscious shaman.

He looked very young, sleep smoothing out the worry lines round his eyes. He also looked very small and very thin. He resembled a schoolboy, not a magician or a protector.

"That bloke needs a few square meals," Merrick observed. "And a new suit. And about a week in bed."

"I was thinking along those lines myself," Crane said.

"I bet you were."

"Shut up. I've no idea how he can be that poor. Twenty guineas for a night's work, and another thirty for this excursion. But that suit's threadbare."

"Blood under his nails, as well, right in. Wasn't just leaning on it."

"Yes, I noticed that. What do you think?"

"Same as you, I reckon."

"Ye-es. The question is, is he up to the job?"

Merrick made a face. "Don't ask me. I got no idea what he can do, and no idea what the job is anyway. The last time I knew this much fuck all, we was on a boat to China."

"And now we're going back to Piper," said Crane. "And on the whole, I'd rather be in Shanghai."

Chapter Six

There was an extremely old carriage waiting for them at Lychdale station. It had a faded coat of arms on the side and half a dozen magpies perched on the roof. The coachman gave an unenthusiastic grunt as the three men emerged from the station and made a token effort to help with the bags before whipping up the horses.

Stephen grabbed the edge of the seat as the coach began to move. "Is this thing not sprung?"

"No. Absolutely nothing in this place is conducive to comfort," said Crane. "The house is decaying, the furnishings are museum pieces, half the staff are consumed with loathing of me out of loyalty to my father, or because I remind them of my brother. In any case, they're people who lived in the same house as Hector when there are perfectly good ditches to die in, which tells you as much as you need to know. Nobody within thirty miles of Piper can cook. And you can thank your lucky stars for the weather, I doubt we'll need more than four or five fires to make the place tolerable of an evening."

"Well, some cool would be a respite." Stephen fiddled with the ancient catch in an attempt to pull down the window. "It's very hot."

"Piper will be damned cold," said Crane. "If we find a witch, we should definitely burn her."

It was a good half hour's drive in the most uncomfortable carriage Stephen had ever encountered. Crane and Merrick both settled into a sort of traveller's trance, eyes shut, minds inactive, getting through an unpleasant journey by reducing mental engagement to a minimum.

Stephen was hot and jolted, wearisomely tired after his nap on the train but without a chance of sleeping, and his hands were increasingly uncomfortable. The train journey had been unpleasant, naturally, but that was the iron of the carriages surrounding him. This was ambient, in the ether; it was old and awkward and dry like a scab, and it was getting stronger as they drove.

When they reached Piper, Stephen began to see what it was.

He stood in front of the house and stared at it. Piper was a substantial Jacobean building in grey stone, with small panelled windows sitting in the thick walls like deep-set eyes. The front was hung thickly with ivy, and the woods encroached too closely on what had once been elegant gardens. The gravelled drive was pierced by weeds. Magpies screeched and cawed in the trees, and a trio of the birds strutted in front of the three men.

"Three for a funeral," he muttered. "This is a mausoleum."

Crane glanced at him but didn't ask for an explanation. Stephen wouldn't have given one anyway. The etheric flow round the house was an abnormal trickle, the woods pounded in his consciousness far more than he'd expected, and there was a dreadful sense of something pent up, bottled for years, brooding.

"Dormant," he said, mostly to himself. "Or dead. Too long asleep to wake. Coma."

"You're being a little unnerving," said Crane. "Are you going to tell me there's a beautiful princess sleeping in the tower room?"

"That wouldn't be my first guess." Stephen pushed his hands through his too-short hair. "Have you seen the mummies at the British Museum?"

"The Egyptian ones? No, not yet. But they have a similar thing in China."

"Did you ever imagine if they started moving? Withered hands reaching towards you and sunken eyes staring?"

"I didn't, but now I know what I'll be dreaming about tonight."

"It's how this house feels." Stephen was compulsively flexing and pulling at his fingers. "I suppose we should go in," he added without enthusiasm.

Crane led the way. An elderly bald man was standing at the thick wood door, his heavy jowls conveying weary disgust. "Your lordship," he mumbled.

"Graham. This is Mr. Day, who is attending to some legal matters for me. I'll expect you and your staff to answer all his questions as fully as possible."

The butler looked Stephen up and down. He didn't roll his eyes and turn away in contempt, but it was evidently a close-run thing.

"Yes, my lord." Graham bowed them in. "Mr. Skewton has left a number of papers for your lordship on your lordship's desk in your lordship's study. And Sir James and Lady Thwaite have left cards for your lordship, your lordship."

Crane looked at him expressionlessly. Graham stared back.

"Very good," said Crane finally. "Mr. Merrick is of course responsible while I'm in residence. Do take the opportunity to rest your feet, Graham."

The old man's bald head flushed a dark red. "*I* don't neglect my duty, your lordship. Lord Crane would never have suggested such a thing. The maids have put your guest in the Blue Room, your lordship, but I dare say Merrick will have something to say about that on your lordship's behalf. The Peony Room, perhaps."

He stalked off through the hall towards the servants' quarters. Merrick followed, soft footed. A door down a corridor slammed, almost certainly in Merrick's face.

"Loyal family retainer?" asked Stephen.

"That's right."

"Couldn't you pension him off?"

"Too much effort. If I got a decent butler, I'd have to import an entire competent household to support him, and since I'm going to sell this damned barrack as soon as I've unpicked the legal situation and clarified the accounts, I can't summon up the energy."

"Oh, you're selling the house?"

"Or setting fire to it," said Crane. "I'm currently leaning that way."

"It's very cold," Stephen agreed, looking around. Darkly panelled walls, heavy wooden furniture, old hangings and threadbare rugs... "Forgive my curiosity, but I thought your family was rich."

"It is," said Crane. "There are extensive landholdings round here and the land is good. Hector was expensive, and Griffin was stealing with both hands, but there's plenty of money. But one of the ways the rich stay rich is by not spending anything."

"I knew I was doing something wrong. What was the significance of that exchange about rooms?"

"Don't ask."

"Well," said Stephen, rubbing his arms and feeling grateful for his jacket for the first time that day, "perhaps I could look round and familiarise myself with the place?" *And see if I can work out what's wrong with it,* he added mentally.

"I'll take you round," said Crane. "Neither Skewton nor the Thwaites offer the charm of your company, and I'm saying that to a man who spent the night disembowelling cats."

"I did *not*—"

"This is the drawing room. It probably wouldn't be so bad without the panelling, or the chairs, and if it was in a different house."

Stephen followed Crane round the chilling, ancient house, mentally mapping it without effort, half listening to Crane's sardonic commentary as he tried to pinpoint the source of his discomfort.

Magpies everywhere. They were carved in wood and stone, perched over lintels, etched into metal, in paint and paper and embroidery. He made a protesting noise at a particularly ugly group in china, arrayed along a mantelpiece.

"Aren't they just," Crane agreed. "My great-aunt supplied them. She'd constantly warn us not to play with them, as though any boy in his right mind would."

"Was she responsible for the tapestry-work magpies as well?"

"In the last room? No, I've no idea who that was. Some passing bedlamite, perhaps. My grandfather organised the magpie-bearing silverware, as you will see at dinner if Graham hasn't sold it all. From here we can go down to the library or up to the next floor, which is mostly under covers, except for the Long Gallery where we keep the family pictures, and which will make you think better of Great-Aunt Lucie's porcelain birds."

"Library last, please," said Stephen. "Let's try the gallery."

"If you insist. You're looking for something, aren't you?" Crane led the way up stairs whose oak treads were deeply worn.

"I am, but I'm not sure what," Stephen admitted. "There's something very old and odd and quite unpleasant about this house."

"Yes, it's Graham."

Stephen grinned and followed him into the long room.

It was very dusty and, again, very cold. There were a couple of chairs, swathed in holland covers. A few tall windows let in the sunshine, which seemed to lose all its heat on the way through the glass. Above, a long skylight was covered in dead leaves and dirt, so that the room was still somewhat murky. Pictures, framed in gilt and dark wood, hung all the way down.

Stephen stared up at the ceiling. "This could be a lovely room if that skylight was clean." He jumped slightly as something landed on the glass with a thump.

"Bloody magpies," said Crane. "If you cleaned it, they'd just foul it in minutes. Well, here, we are. My father and Hector."

Stephen had never seen the previous Lord Crane. He had seen Hector Vaudrey on the terrible night when he had come to their house. He had been just twelve, and his mother had sent him to his room at once, but he remembered the red face, the smell of drink, the voices.

He made himself look at the full-length portrait. A bulky, grey-haired elderly man stood next to a large, well-built, golden-blond man in his thirties. Stephen remembered him from the vantage point of a terrified child, as a giant, and given the way the painted figure towered over his father, he guessed Hector must have been a similar height to his younger brother, perhaps three inches over six feet, though much broader in the shoulders.

Hector was staring out of the portrait with a slight sneer on his finely shaped mouth, and a set to his jaw that suggested command, and not a kindly sort. Stephen detected cruelty in his face, nothing in the old lord's neutral gaze. Behind them, two magpies perched on an apple tree.

Stephen glanced round. Crane was watching him. "Is this a good likeness?" he asked, for something to say.

"Probably. Hector got fat, I'm told. This one here is my father as a boy. He kept the magpie as a pet. The next one is him with my grandmother—"

"Is this in chronological order?"

"Yes, pretty much."

"There's not one of you, or your mother?"

"There was a family portrait from when I was a baby, but my father took it down. It's in the attic."

"Oh. Did she die?"

"No." Crane started to stroll down the line of paintings. "She left my father when I was a year old. I've no idea what happened to her."

Stephen stood still for a moment, so that he had to hurry after Crane. "Did you never see her again?"

"No, how should I? This is Great-Aunt Lucie. Fear her. My grandfather, just before his death."

"Really?" The picture showed a mere youth, wearing a waistcoat embroidered with magpies.

"Yes, my father was posthumous."

"They all keep up the magpie theme in the paintings," Stephen observed.

"Tradition," said Crane, without interest. "Although putting them on one's waistcoat really is the outside of enough. This is the third earl, the second didn't live long either. Here's the first—this is the only good painting in the room if you ask me. Feel free to comment on what a handsome devil he is. Then the next—Mr. Day?"

Stephen was standing in front of the first Earl Crane, staring, the astonishment so powerful it held him completely still. The recognition was instant, and now he saw the picture, and compared it to the man next to him, he couldn't believe it hadn't struck him earlier.

"My God," he said. "I am so stupid."

"Are you all right?" enquired Crane, cautiously.

Stephen licked his lips. "I've seen him before."

"Well, you've seen me," said Crane. "And the resemblance is quite strong."

"No. I've seen that picture. Or rather, a reproduction, an engraving." Stephen shook his head, incredulous. "You said he was the first Earl Crane. So, before that, your family title was Fortunegate?"

"It was. And still is, actually. I'm Viscount Fortunegate too." Stephen couldn't find words for that. Crane contemplated him with amusement. "I wish I'd known that would give you so much pleasure. I'd have saved it for a special occasion."

"You're Lord Fortunegate. Your *ancestor* was Lord Fortunegate."

"That's how it works. Are you going to tell me why you care?"

Stephen indicated the painting. It was a large gilt-framed oil work showing a man whose lean build and patrician features gave him a distinct resemblance to the current Lord Crane. His long-fingered hand rested on a window ledge on which, inevitably, a magpie perched, adorned with a carved gold ring on which the painter had lavished detail. More magpies flew in the background of the painting, which showed Piper in well-kept days. It looked gracious, spacious, elegant. A table in the foreground was covered in handwritten papers. The first earl looked out at them with a slight smile on his face.

"That man," Stephen said, "your ancestor, Lord Fortunegate...he was a magician. Specifically, he was one of the most powerful magicians this country has ever known. He...good God, he *invented* modern practice, he shaped our society as it stands today. His book of theory—that picture's in the frontispiece—"

"Wait." Crane had a hand up. "Stop. My great-great-etcetera grandfather was—like you?"

"I *wish* I was like him," Stephen said. "He was one of the great practitioners and the great lawmakers."

Crane stared at the painting. "Well, that's something I didn't expect. Is it hereditary?"

"Talent? A bit. You get family lines sometimes, but rather crooked ones. My aunt's a witch, for example." Stephen glanced at Crane. "But there's obviously something come down in the blood. Do you know how most people refer to him, the name he used?"

"Go on."

"He was the Magpie Lord. And, of course, that explains the magpie compulsion."

"The what?"

Stephen strolled down the length of the gallery, looking at the older paintings. "These go back a while. And not a magpie in any of them. I wonder if the Magpie Lord renamed the house?"

"I could probably find out. So?"

"So since the Magpie Lord, you've all been frantically filling the house with magpies. Carvings and cutlery and appalling porcelain..."

"It's the family symbol."

"Look at the paintings. It wasn't the family symbol before the Magpie Lord. Did you never wonder why a family titled Crane would use a magpie for a symbol?"

"It occurred to me fairly forcibly when I had my tattoos," Crane said. "Unlike magpies, cranes are common in China. And a lot easier to ink."

Stephen shook his head. "You hate your family. You loathe this house. You were five thousand miles away and never coming back. You could have chosen any design you liked. And you *still* felt compelled to etch magpies into approximately a quarter of your skin."

"It was a whim." Crane sounded slightly defensive.

"How long did it take, start to finish?"

"Three years or so, but—"

"Quite a whim. I bet they hurt, too."

"I chose to have my tattoos," said Crane, with a flare of anger that took Stephen by surprise. "*I* chose them. I don't know what you're suggesting but I didn't get them done at the command of some long-dead warlock—"

"*He was not a warlock!*"

The words rang off the gallery walls. Stephen didn't care. "The Magpie Lord was one of the greatest figures of our history. He was utterly intolerant of abuse of power. He was one of the

60

legislators who codified the law on practitioners, establishing just how we govern ourselves, specifically to prevent warlocks hurting the innocent. And magpies were a key part of his power in some way that I don't pretend to understand, and the people who carry his bloodline and live in his house have been picking up that resonance for *two hundred years* after his death, and I think your *choice* to have those tattoos was driven by that resonance, and frankly I would be proud to be touched by the Magpie Lord, even so remotely. Is that clearer?"

Crane was leaning against the wall, watching him. His eyes dwelled appreciatively on Stephen's face. They no longer looked angry, but amused, and held a distinct touch of speculation.

Stephen took a deep breath. "And you have no idea what I'm talking about and don't know what a warlock is," he continued, in a more normal voice. "Sorry. I'm rather an admirer of his, that's all."

And the atmosphere of Piper was nagging at him, draining, dry, oppressive, like a constant itch behind the eyes.

Crane's lips curled, eyes still on Stephen's face. Maybe in China one could keep staring at another person for a long time and it wouldn't seem out of place, Stephen thought. He could feel the colour rising in his cheeks, and he suddenly wished he'd found out more before coming here: why Lucien Vaudrey had been thrown out by his father, and exactly what the whispers of scandal surrounding his name were.

Crane was still watching him, with that lazy, speculative smile broadening on his tanned, aristocratic, handsome face, and Stephen realised that he was watching him right back, staring at the man like an idiot girl.

Oh, no. Absolutely not. Don't even think about it.

He turned abruptly, looking back up the gallery, and glimpsed Hector Vaudrey's painted face. "I'll go to the library now," he said, making his voice neutral. "This is a wonderful discovery, and I would very much like to find out more, later, but it's not relevant to the immediate problem of the Judas jack."

As he spoke, he headed back the way they had come. Crane caught up after a few steps and led the way down the stairs.

"It's down here. Will you want me in there?"

"Actually, I'd appreciate it if you'd stay well away till I give you the word. Can you go and be with Mr. Merrick while I do this, just in case?"

"In case?" Crane frowned. "Is that standard professional caution, or are you concerned about something?"

"I don't know yet," Stephen said. "I'll go and find out."

Chapter Seven

Crane watched the heavy panelled door close behind Day. He'd seen the man brace himself before going in, registered the expression of distaste on his face, wondered what strange sensitivities were being triggered.

Crane was not so much a brave man as an obstinate one. He had endured experiences that made him nauseous with remembered fear or pain when he looked back at them, because at the time it never seemed possible to back down. He would not have backed down now.

But he was extremely glad that Day hadn't asked him to go in the library.

An odd little man, that. Too thin, too pale, but his sharp features were appealing, and when his tawny eyes had been lit by animation, he had suddenly seemed very striking indeed. Passion would definitely improve Stephen Day, Crane thought.

Not one to pursue, though, despite a moment's temptation back in the gallery. The man seemed to be living on his nerves, tense and twitchy, and Crane needed him to do his job. And that momentary flash of rabbit-in-a-snare panic in his eyes suggested inexperience, and it had been a long time since Crane had found that anything more than a chore. Still...

He put the thought aside for consideration and wandered off to find Merrick, who was in the master bedroom, attending to the unpacking.

"What's going on?" Crane enquired in Shanghainese. Graham was a chronic eavesdropper, so they avoided English for even the most trivial conversations, mostly to annoy.

"Nothing's going on, this is the countryside. Where's the shaman?"

"Library," said Crane, seating himself on the edge of the ancient, eternally damp four-poster. "Doing shaman things. Guess what I just learned about my honourable ancestors."

He gave Merrick a highly coloured account of the revelations about the first Earl Crane. Merrick stopped folding shirts and propped himself against the chest of drawers to listen. "Well, there you are," he said at last. "What's it all mean, then?"

"No idea. Nothing probably, but it made the shaman happy for a brief moment. Where have you put him?"

"Peony Room." Merrick returned his attention to the shirts, which he continued to straighten in the silence that followed, ignoring Crane's folded arms and raised eyebrow.

"Peony Room," said Crane, since Merrick wasn't rising to it. "The old man won, did he?"

"I let him win. Seemed like a good idea."

"Because?"

"Because it puts the shaman next to you at night, with a connecting door, not down the other end of a corridor, out of earshot."

Crane glared at him. "And if the old bastard goes round telling everyone that the shaman is here to keep my bed warm?"

"That's the shaman's problem." Merrick slammed a drawer shut. "He's here to keep you safe. If he doesn't like it..."

"If the blood-covered sorcerer who can bend metal by looking at it doesn't like it," Crane said, "then what, exactly?"

There was a triple rap at the half-open door. Merrick's eyes flicked over, and his face set. Crane sighed silently.

"Come in, Mrs. Mitching."

Piper's housekeeper was a grim-faced woman in her early forties, who tackled everything with an air of humourless irritation. Crane approved of her, since she made no secret of her contempt for his father and brother, and she returned his approval because, whatever people said about him, he kept his hands off her girls.

Crane loathed servant-hall politics as much as any other kind, but he made sure there was no trace of boredom or irritation in his voice as he enquired what he could do for her.

Mrs. Mitching hesitated, which was unusual. "Well. My lord. Well, I wouldn't bring this to you, but... Graham says it's nonsense, but he hasn't looked or listened and... My girls aren't stupid, my lord. Elsa Brook might not be book-learned and she has fancies but she's no fool. And the fact is, it won't do, and we don't have to put up with it, and we won't."

"Then you shan't," said Crane promptly. "Can you tell me what it is you won't put up with, and perhaps I can help?"

Mrs. Mitching bit her lip. "The fact is, my lord... I wouldn't say anything—with all said and done, I don't want to speak ill—but Elsa Brook and Jane Diver both... I saw it myself, my lord. There's no getting away from it. I *saw* it."

"What did you see?" said Crane, as patiently as possible.

Mrs. Mitching took a deep breath. "Mr. Hector, my lord. We've all seen Mr. Hector."

"You've seen Mr. Hector," Crane repeated.

"Yes, my lord."

"Mr. Hector, who is dead."

"*Yes*, my lord," said Mrs. Mitching. "And that's not all of it."

In the library, Stephen blinked and stretched and flexed his aching hands as he brought his attention back from the etheric flow, such as it was, and into the world again. His head hurt, he was extremely cold, and he was painfully hungry, which came as no surprise, given how lifeless the house was. The etheric currents that he normally drew from without thinking were shallow trickles here.

How had such a deathly house been the Magpie Lord's home? Or perhaps that was why it was lifeless, perhaps he'd drained it in some way.

He stared at his knucklebones, white under the skin, and the image of mummies popped into his head again, irritatingly. This house wasn't a dead thing moving, it was a live thing dying. Or perhaps the image simply meant the shrivelled corpse of something once powerful.

He rose from his crouching position on the floor and looked round the room as he rolled his shoulders. It should have been a lovely place, a double-height room with dark wood shelving, filled with books, many leather-bound and ancient. He should have been consumed with excitement at the idea that somewhere in there might be the Magpie Lord's own books.

But the room was dusty and loveless and lifeless, and filled with the ivy stink of the Judas jack, and the echoes of two men's desperate, self-hating, lonely deaths, and the very recent shadows of Crane's fear and pain, and it made his hands hurt.

"The blazes with this," he muttered to himself, and headed for the door, which he pulled open only to be confronted with a raised fist on the other side.

"Oh, there you are, I was just about to knock," said Crane brightly. "I have a *fascinating* story for you."

Crane sat back in an uncomfortably embroidered chair and watched the show with interest.

Mrs. Mitching had been extremely reluctant to repeat her story to Day, despite Crane's assurances that he could, in some unspecified way, shed light on the mystery. But she had produced a pot of tea and a plate of heavy, wet cake and solid, indigestible buns, and to Crane's frank astonishment Day had devoured two slices of cake and three buns with enthusiasm that had worked better than any flattery, as well as obviously genuine interest in her tale, and now Mrs. Mitching was as close to relaxing as anyone so rigid ever could.

"So let me be sure I understand," Day said. "All the...incidents happened in the Rose Walk. You and Miss Diver saw him from a distance, seeming to rage and hit out at something."

"That's right, sir."

"And he came up to Miss Brook and spoke to her. Shouted at her."

"But she couldn't hear a word, just saw his mouth moving."

"And when she ran, he chased her to the edge of the Rose Walk..."

"And grabbed at her dress, sir, she says. She swears it was him clutching at her skirts, and that the grip came loose as she stepped off the end of the Rose Walk onto the paved path. With all the rose bushes along there, it's no surprise to me if something did catch at her skirt, and it's no surprise what she'd think either, the way that man carried on—begging your pardon, my lord."

"Not at all."

"Had he, ah, chased Miss Brook in life?" asked Day. "Or is there any reason why she might feel pursued when you and Miss Diver didn't?"

"Elsa Brook is imaginative," said Mrs. Mitching, much as she might have said, *Elsa Brook is leprous.* "She does her job well and she's no trouble but she has fancies."

"Do you think this was a fancy?" Day asked seriously.

Mrs. Mitching hesitated. "Maybe, sir. I know what I saw, and Jane Diver isn't imaginative, and I wouldn't blame Brook that she was frit after what she saw, or that she feared something was coming after her..."

Day's tawny eyes were fixed on Mrs. Mitching's face. "But?" he asked softly.

Silence. At last she spoke, in an unwilling rush. "You couldn't trust Mr. Hector in life, and I don't trust him in death either, and that's the truth, sir. And none of my girls are going into the Rose Walk again."

Day leaned back. "That's probably wise."

"What do you think sir?" demanded Mrs. Mitching. "Is it really Mr. Hector? My lord says as you know about these things."

"I explained that you've come across some odd things in the course of your work," Crane put in, as Day's eyes flicked to him.

"I have," Day agreed. "Learned opinion holds that hauntings are just...shadows, like visible echoes, important or terrible events being played out again and again, without substance, like Chinese lantern shows. Very frightening, very uncomfortable for you, but not dangerous. Just a ripple in time, a meaningless repetition that will ebb away."

His voice was soothing. Mrs. Mitching nodded slowly. "A ripple in time," she repeated. "Well, I never."

"If I had to guess," Day added, "I'd say that Miss Brook might well have reacted to a very frightening experience with understandable panic. As you say, clothes do catch on rose bushes. I shouldn't think it at all likely that there is anything to pose a danger to anyone. That said, you should still keep your staff away from the Rose Walk. These things seem to become more...fixed if people see them and believe in them, and I don't suppose Lord Crane wants to be haunted by the image of his late brother."

"In that, you are correct. The Rose Walk is out of bounds as of this moment." Crane tapped a finger on the table for emphasis. "Nobody sets foot there on pain of dismissal. Please advise your staff, Mrs. Mitching, and I'll tell Merrick to pass the word."

He ushered the housekeeper out with thanks for her loyalty. The door shut behind her. Both men were silent for a few seconds as her footsteps moved away.

Crane said softly, "Anything in it?"

Day was rubbing his hands together, pulling at the joints. "I'm afraid there may be. She's totally earthbound—that is, she's not someone I would expect to pick up the kind of currents and images I talked about. And she believed what she said. She and Miss Diver saw something, the sensitive Miss Brook experienced something much stronger and more menacing. And possibly physical."

"You don't think Brook just caught her skirt on a rose bush?"

"I hope she did," said Day grimly. "If she didn't, you have a very serious problem. I'm wondering if this is the source of what's so badly wrong in this house."

"So when you said there was no danger..."

"That may have been true. Or it may not."

The trader in Crane made a mental note that Day was a fluent and unrepentant liar, even as he picked at a loose thread on the embroidered chair with the edge of a fingernail. "Is it your professional opinion that the ghost of my brother attempted to rape my housemaid? Is that actually possible?"

"I won't know what it is, or what it can do, till I see it. Physical manifestation isn't common, so hopefully it'll all come down to the usual ingredients of a haunting: imagination and indigestion. Failing that, it's most likely to be the echo in time I described. But failing *that*..." Day pulled a face, stuffed his hands in his pockets and walked over to the window. "This isn't a happy house."

Crane joined him, looking out at what should have been a beautiful vista of lawns in spring. The grass was long and rank, the trees crowding in. A magpie landed outside the window and cawed offensively, and there was a flurry of black and white and blue as a crowd of them settled on the grass.

"Five—no, six. Six for hell." Day leaned on the window frame. "They were murdered. Your father and brother, I mean. It was the Judas jack, no question about it. I don't want you to set foot in the library till I've had a chance to...fumigate it, if you see what I mean."

Crane nodded. "Very well. What about Hector?"

"Don't give it a name, we don't know what it is yet," said Day. "I think I need to be on the Rose Walk tonight. Can you make sure nobody else is there? And I may need some supplies, just in case there is something to deal with."

"What sort of supplies? I'm not sure we have holy water. Or eye of newt."

"I had in mind salt and iron filings, and I'd appreciate it if you could avoid the Macbeth jokes."

"That comes up a lot, does it?"

"Now and then."

"Merrick will arrange everything," said Crane. "When do we start? What do we do?"

"We?"

"We. This is my house and it's supposedly my brother back from the grave. I think that makes it my problem."

"Yes, but keeping you safe is my job. Really, don't come. It'll be tedious or unpleasant, and possibly both. I never do hauntings if I can avoid them."

"Do you want to avoid this one?" asked Crane. "I made an assumption this was your business, but if not, it's easy enough to keep people away from the Rose Walk—"

Day was waving a hand to stop him. "No, not at all, it is my business. If there's any chance of a malignant entity, I have a responsibility to stop it before it does any harm."

"Well, I feel the same," said Crane. "And you didn't sign up to face Hector. Ah, Mr. Day?" he said over Day's protest. "I'm a Shanghai Joe. I don't care how magical you are, you're not winning an argument with me unless I let you. I'll tell Merrick to put the word out and he'll come to you for a list."

Chapter Eight

The Rose Walk was a long stone pergola through what had once been an ornamental garden. Its roses were bursting into bloom early thanks to the sultry, unseasonable April heat, about which it had been all too easy to forget inside Piper's clammy walls. It was twilight now. The waning moon was up, the stars were coming out, and Day and Crane strolled through the shadowy grounds towards the long stone walkway, inhaling the night perfumes of flowers and greenery and clean air, laughing.

The evening had been awkward at first. They had eaten in the huge dining room, at the massive oak table, surrounded by portraits of Vaudreys gone, and Day—small, shabby, poor—had looked utterly out of place, and obviously felt it, among the faded ancestral magnificence, as had doubtless been Graham's intention. Crane, cursing himself for not ordering the meal somewhere less formal, had set himself to put the man at his ease, since God knew this was uncomfortable enough already, and a chance remark about gambling sharps had led to Day's admission that he had a certain knack with cards. So Crane had produced a pack, and Day had made it sit up and beg. He took a shuffled pack, shuffled twice more, and spread the cards out in suit and number order; shuffled twice more and brought all the face cards together; sent the cards flying from one hand to another in a series of elaborate twisting switchbacks.

Crane had opened another bottle out of respect for the miraculous display, and what had followed was without doubt the most pleasant hour he had ever spent in Piper. Manipulating the cards had visibly relaxed Day, so that he spoke freely about some of his work, and they had ended up exchanging ever more absurd stories, of smuggling and bizarre magical crimes and life in China, killing the second bottle in the process. The wine, Crane noticed, had no effect at all on Day's small frame.

The evening had become, in fact, ridiculously enjoyable, and Crane found himself increasingly intrigued by the man who sat opposite him, and decidedly annoyed when they had broken off to search for his brother's perturbed spirit.

Stephen Day had a keen mind and a puckish sense of humour, with a relish for the absurd. He also had an infectious sideways grin, his top lip catching on a crooked canine tooth, which gave him a foxy look that Crane was rapidly coming to find highly provocative. And the quick flashing light in those tawny-gold eyes had caused Crane to reassess his ideas about inexperience: there was definitely more to Day than he'd thought. It was, Crane reflected, a pity his small, sinewy body was so scrawny, although that in itself was a mystery.

"A pleasant night for a postprandial stroll and a spot of ghost-hunting," Crane remarked now. "Some time you really must tell me how anyone who eats as much as you stays so thin."

"I know, I know," Day said. "I'm eating like a, a—"

"Starving vulture."

"Thank you. Yes. It's the house. I'm used to much more lively environments."

"Aren't we all?"

"In terms of power, I mean. I can't draw on any etheric flow, any power in the house, which means I'm stripping myself every time I do anything. Which is to say, burning energy from within myself. As you do when you take physical exercise, but more so."

"Is that safe?"

"Oh yes, as long as you have plenty to eat and drink. If you don't, or you try to do too much, it burns fat and then muscle, and eventually bone and brain and skin." They reached the side of the Rose Walk and, in unspoken concord, turned to walk alongside it. "I stripped myself to the bone last winter," Day went on, "and very unpleasant it was too. I'm still recovering from that, actually."

Convalescent, thought Crane. That explained a lot. He bit back an absurd urge to ask if Day really ought to be working. "What were you doing last winter?"

"Hunting a murderer. On Romney Marshes, which is an etheric sinkhole—nothing to draw on, worse than here. I spent twelve of the nastiest hours of my life playing tag with a killer, around a marsh, in the dark, on my own, trying not to die."

"Did you catch him? Was he one of you, a practitioner?"

"A warlock. And yes, I found him. I stripped myself well beyond anything I'd have chanced if I hadn't been fighting for my life. I woke up looking like something out of the Egyptian Room at the British Museum, and weighing about five stone. I couldn't walk for a month. Lost all my hair. It was vile."

"So who won?" Crane said. "It doesn't sound like it was you." They had reached the end of the Rose Walk. Day peered down it, crossed the end and led the way down the other side, still outside it.

"No, I won," he said. "I woke up."

Crane whistled. "I thought I had an adventurous life. Pitched magical battles on Romney Marshes..."

"Have absolutely nothing to recommend them."

They paced on.

"What's etheric flow?"

"The ether is...a kind of energy that runs through everything. Through the air, through living things, in greater or lesser quantities. It carries, well, magic."

"Like *ch'i*?"

"Like what?"

"*Ch'i*. Life force. A sort of energy flow that permeates everything and links the world together."

"Yes! Exactly. Is that Chinese? Did you learn that from your shaman?"

"It's a basic principle of Chinese culture." Crane watched Day's face with amusement. "Really. Children learn about it. It's part of medicine. It's completely normal, everyone knows it exists."

"Really? So..." They had reached the other end of the Rose Walk, which opened up into an overgrown lawn with a statueless stone plinth at its centre. Day glanced down the passage. "That's fascinating and I'd love to know more, but I think I need to go in if I'm to have a chance of seeing anything. You don't have to."

"We established that I do," Crane said mildly. "Can we talk while we wait for visitations?"

"Let's walk the ground," Day suggested. "Speak up if you feel anything uncomfortable or strange. It's entirely possible that nothing whatsoever will happen and we'll just stay out here getting cold."

Feet echoed on stone as they paced down the dark walk, Crane limiting his long stride to the shorter man's, skin tingling as he listened for whatever there might be to hear. He felt a quiver of nerves as his sleeve snagged on something, and laughed at himself for a fool almost at once as he brushed away the tendrils of rose.

Day's face was sharp and intent in the moonlight, hands out, fingers moving gently, like a pianist imagining music. Crane paced by his side, turned when he turned, and took a breath when he relaxed.

"Absolutely nothing," Day said. "I'm becoming hopeful this was just Miss Brook's imagination after all. If we sit on that bench, will it collapse under both our weight?"

"Probably." Crane tested it. "Maybe not. So is that how it works, you draw on the flow, the *ch'i*, to do magic?"

"More or less, yes."

Crane contemplated that. The stone bench was cold under his legs, and there was a chilly breeze rustling the rose bushes. Day shifted on the bench, curling a leg underneath himself, stretching his hands reflexively. Crane could feel his warmth, very close.

"Can you, ah, *strip* other people?" he asked idly, and felt Day become suddenly still in the darkness.

"Why do you ask?"

"There was a...they called it a plague," Crane said. "Bodies found looking like, well, Egyptian mummies. Dead. Someone I knew, and had seen two days previously in perfect health, turned up in his bed apparently starved to death. The authorities said it was a plague. The locals said it was a *chiang-shih*, a...damn, what's the word? Walking corpses that drink blood."

"Vampire?"

"That's it. But Yu Len insisted it was *wugu*. Harmful magic. A bad shaman. And from what you just said about stripping yourself..."

"Yes. Well, you're right, or rather, your shaman knew his business. You can strip other people, or drain them in a number of ways. But it's utterly illegal. Wrong. It's more or less the definition of a warlock. Any idea what happened?"

"It stopped eventually. I heard someone had decapitated a corpse in the cemetery which was thought to be the culprit." Crane looked round. "I'm now waiting for you to tell me there's no such thing as walking corpses."

"I'm sure you are," Day said, and gave his snag-toothed grin as Crane shot him a look. "Let's just say you're unlikely to meet one."

The garden at the end of the long dark passage was a soft grey of waving grass in the moonlight, with the empty plinth squat in its centre, framed by the solid stone pillars of the pergola. Crane wondered what Day saw.

"Since we could be here for a while, and you did say it was a long story, would you tell me about the tattoos?" Day said. "Specifically, about being forced to have one. I've been wondering about that for days."

It was an involved story, veering between farcical and exciting, and Crane knew he told it well. He couldn't see the smaller man's face as clearly as he'd have liked, but the shaman was rocking with laughter in the darkness as Crane reached a height of absurdity, making the old stone bench wobble alarmingly. Crane straightened a long leg to brace a foot against the ground, glanced down the passageway, and sucked in a sharp breath that cut off Day's laughter instantly as he whipped round to look.

The Rose Walk was completely dark, the thick overgrown brambles that wound over and around it cutting off the moonlight, but the figure walking up it was as visible as if it were day. He wasn't glowing, he was simply there, easily seen, solid.

He was Hector Vaudrey.

Crane jerked backwards on the bench. His hand found Day's, and he involuntarily gripped it, feeling the instant sharp needling of his skin as a comfort. Day's fingers closed on his, and Crane heard his rapid, shallow breathing.

Hector was much, much older now. When Crane had last seen him, he was a handsome man in his early twenties. The portrait showed him just a few years later. The figure that reeled and stumbled up the stone path was ageing—still solidly built, but fat replacing muscle, his face lined and pouchy.

And he was insane, it seemed. He shouted silently at nothing Crane could see, raging and cursing, hands grasping the air, thrashing, plucking at his collar, grabbing his hair and pulling it down hard around his temples. He kicked and jerked angrily, stumbling as much sideways as forward.

He was coming towards them. Crane's entire body cringed away. He couldn't breathe. His fingers tightened convulsively on Day's.

"Keep calm," Day whispered, gently extricating his hand. "Stay here."

The thing that looked like Hector staggered up the path, fingers dragging at his ears. He put both hands to his neck and seemed to start trying to twist his head off.

Day rose and stepped forward, the bag of salt and iron filings in his hand. Crane took a pace to stand next to him.

"Stay *back*," Day hissed, irritated.

"No," said Crane. He spoke as quietly as Day had, but Hector's head snapped up at the sound. The pale blue eyes that Crane remembered so well focused on him, and the cruel light in them hadn't changed in two decades. Hector strode forward, suddenly in full control, his face distorted with rage, screaming words that were very nearly audible.

"Get out of here," said Day urgently. "Go!"

Crane didn't move, couldn't. Hector's arms were out, reaching for him, and the big hands were the size of hams now. He was visibly growing, towering in his consuming rage.

"Stop there, shadow," Day snarled, stepping quickly in front of Crane, and flung a handful of glittering white dust at the advancing figure. Hector shook his head, batted at the air in front of him as though clearing cobwebs, kept walking.

"You're making it stronger. *Go.*" Day reached for another handful of salt and iron from the bag, and Hector hit him, a backhander that somehow connected, knocked him off his feet and sent him reeling back into the roses that lined the path on both sides, trapping them.

"*Run!*" Day screamed, and there was real alarm in his voice now as he struggled to extricate himself from the grasping tangle of thorns.

Crane could barely hear him over Hector's bellows. The dead man, his brother, the monster of his youth loomed over him, roaring the loathing of years, spitting out all the old hate and contempt and cruel promises, seasoned now with bitter, overwhelming resentment. *My land, my inheritance, my life, you stole it, you filth.* His face was dark and mottled with rage, and his jaw was open too wide, cracking, teeth huge pale tombstones in the gaping mouth that lunged forward to devour Crane with darkness.

Crane took a single step to meet his brother and punched him square in the face.

There was a moment of connection as his fist unquestionably met something. Then there was nothing to stop his forward momentum, and he was stumbling right into the monstrous vision, except that the great thing was also reeling back, grabbing at its face.

Its head fell off.

It bounced twice and rolled gently away, coming to rest on its side. The face looked like Hector again, like a human rather than an ogre, and it was weeping.

The headless body staggered and fell to its knees, arms out, patting blindly at the stone. A searching hand fell onto the mass of golden hair by chance. The body hoisted its sobbing head up in the air, positioning it over the stump of neck, ready to put it back on.

"No, you do *not,*" said Day, standing over the grotesque pieta. He ripped open the bag of salt and iron as he spoke, with his fingers in an odd, clawlike position. The white and grey dust hung in the air above the Hector thing for a few unnatural seconds. Day's fingers stabbed downwards, and the dust descended with intense force, like monsoon rain—

And Hector wasn't there.

Crane stood and stared at the empty stone floor. He felt the sharp prickle of Day's hand on his arm.

"Come on, out of here. I've no idea how long that will keep it away. Walk. Left leg. Right. Left. Come on."

Crane made himself walk. They emerged into the moonlight, out of the rose-lined path, and Crane took a deep, shuddering breath.

"The next time I say *run,*" Day said, "listen to me. Please."

"I'll listen the next time you say not to come at all. Jesus Christ. I need to sit down."

Day looked round quickly, and half-pulled him over to a square stone that had once been a statue's pedestal. Crane sat heavily on the rough stone and slumped forward, resting his forearms on his thighs to support himself.

"I need your left hand." Day squatted down next to him.

Crane extended it without asking. Day took it, brushing his thumb over Crane's knuckles. A pale yellow light from nowhere illuminated the skin.

"What the—"

"Me, that's just me," Day said hastily. "Sorry. I need to see."

"What's that on my hand?"

Day's thumb slid over the dead white patch on his knuckles. "It's an abreaction. You've heard of people's hair turning white when they see a ghost? Like that. It shouldn't be permanent if I can deal with it now. Otherwise it'll just be a white patch. Nothing to worry about." His thumb moved back and forth, gentle but firm, prickling champagne bubbles on Crane's skin.

There was silence for a few moments. Finally Crane forced out, "That thing. Was that Hector? His—his spirit? His soul?"

"I'm not a theologian." Day's hand was folded around Crane's as his thumb slid over the skin, fingertips tingling against Crane's palm. "And this isn't my field. But...it reacted to you, it reacted to your reaction, it was astonishingly physical and close to audible... I think it's not Hector exactly, but it's what's left of him. Or what he is now."

"Marvellous," Crane muttered. "And it's not gone for good?"

"Not yet. I might need help to get rid of it permanently." Day hesitated. "Were you frightened of him, as a child?"

"Terrified. I used to spend half my time in the attic, hiding from him. One holiday he found me and broke my leg in a door so I couldn't run away. It took him three tries. When I heard he was dead, we got drunk for a week."

Day's thumb had stilled, his grip tightening on Crane's hand. "I will make it go away," he said softly. "I'll get rid of it for you. I promise." His thumb resumed its circling movements, slower and a little firmer, warm and close and caressing. "You know," he added, "there are a number of recommended methods of dealing with ghosts—salt and iron, harmonic resonance, some people swear by exorcism, and not just priests—but that's the first time I've seen anyone try a left hook."

"Now you say that," Crane said, "it strikes me that it was a very stupid act."

"It was brave." Day sounded serious. "A bit stupid. But mostly brave."

The shaman knelt before him in the moonlight, painfully close. At some point, Crane wasn't sure when, he'd moved so that his arms were now resting on Crane's thighs, warm and heavy. His hair glimmered dark copper in the cold light, and his caressing thumb was sending spangles of sensation up towards Crane's elbow now.

Crane looked down at him. As if he'd felt the gaze, Day looked up, mouth slightly open, and his wide eyes met Crane's for a long breathless moment.

Crane reached out with his free hand and brushed his thumb slowly over Day's lips, pushing them gently apart, feeling his mouth move softly, opening, accepting the touch. His breath came fast against Crane's hand. Crane's need was suddenly, violently urgent after the night's terror, and Stephen Day was kneeling before him, lips inviting, pupils dilated, a gift to be unwrapped. He pushed his thumb further into the warm mouth and felt a flicker of tongue against his skin, a tentative taste.

"Stephen," said Crane softly, trying out the name.

Stephen tilted his head back a little. "I...I don't..."

"Oh, you do." Crane stroked his fingers possessively over the small chin. "You really do. Lovely boy."

"I'm twenty-eight," Stephen said weakly, and Crane's lips curved, knowing that was surrender.

His hand closed on Stephen's jaw, pulling him closer. "Come here. Unless you want to stay on your knees, of course," he added, with a twitch of a brow, and something in the other man's eyes went suddenly dark.

"Listen to me," Stephen said. "I have been clearing the abreaction for the last few minutes. This has been dull and uneventful, and you're keen to go in and do something more interesting than talk to me. I'm very boring and drab and unattractive, after all, and you'd be much happier talking to Mr. Merrick. You want to forget about me and go in, so you're quite glad to hear that the abreaction has cleared."

"Has it?" said Crane. "Oh, good. Can we go in?"

"Of course," mumbled Stephen. He leaned backwards, shifting his bony elbows off Crane's legs. The moonlight greyed his rather dull, mud-coloured eyes and nondescript features. He looked drawn and tense, almost distressed. Crane didn't know why.

Crane rose and held out a hand. After a second Stephen took it, and Crane heaved him to his feet.

"Ow."

"Did Hector—it—hurt you?" Crane asked.

"No. No, my knees are just a bit stiff. No damage done. Well, I caught my jacket on those roses."

"Merrick is very good at rescuing clothes." They fell into step back through the moon-shadowed grounds to Piper. "He kept me respectable for years. What happens next?"

"I'll walk back the Judas jack tomorrow. See if I can find out where it was made and who did it. Prevent them doing anything else. And then I'll find out what provoked the haunting and make it go away."

"Where to?" Crane asked. "Hector, I mean. Where would he go?"

"I've no idea," said Stephen. "*Away* is really all I'm concerned with. Does it matter?"

Crane shrugged as he opened the side door, and recoiled as he came face to face with Graham, standing right at the door. The old man held a candlestick, and his face was deeply wrinkled and malevolent in the dancing shadows as he looked them both over.

"Oh, there you are, your lordship," he said. "I trust you had a pleasant time in the garden. Dear me, Mr. Day, your lower garments are quite wet. Perhaps you should spend less time on your knees."

He turned on his heel and stalked off. Stephen looked after him, and turned to Crane, face neutral.

"It amuses him to be offensive," Crane said, wondering whether Stephen had grasped the ludicrous insinuation. "My apologies. I'll have a word."

There was nothing in Stephen's muddy eyes, except perhaps tiredness. "Don't bother. Good night."

Chapter Nine

The unseasonable sun was shining through the narrow windows of the drawing room, onto the faded carpets and brocade chairs, and Crane was bored.

Stephen had been particularly uninteresting at breakfast, barely meeting Crane's eyes, making only polite and noncommittal remarks. Crane, deprived of conversation, found his mind kept wandering to Hector, and the jack, and the ghastly legal and financial tangle ahead of him, until he had all but forgotten the dull little man opposite him.

Stephen had disappeared after consuming a huge breakfast and was now sequestered in the library, where he had been all morning, armed with the most detailed map Crane possessed and supplies of tea and cake from Mrs. Mitching. Merrick had gone off to spread the agreed story that the cement fixing the stones of the Rose Walk had deteriorated catastrophically and it was likely to collapse on anyone foolish enough to walk through it. Crane had settled down with Piper's accounts, which possessed all the clarity and order of a plate of *chao mian* noodles but none of the spice, and had thought that this would be the dullest thing he did all day, right up until the moment Sir James and Lady Thwaite arrived to make a morning call.

Sir James concluded his hunting anecdote with a hearty laugh, in which his wife joined. Crane said, "Very good," without any effort at sincerity. "Now…"

"Well." Sir James glanced at his wife. "I expect you're wondering why we're here, my lord, and the fact is, we're having a dinner this evening."

"We had no idea when you'd be back, you see," put in Lady Thwaite. "Or we would have sent you a card. Naturally."

"Cards," said Sir James dismissively. "Man doesn't need a card to share meat with his neighbours. Come and take pot luck with us this evening. You can meet our Helen again, and all the society roundabout here, not to mention the Brutons. Muriel's friends, they are, coming up from London today. Just your sort. Sir Peter and Elise, that's Lady Bruton, don't know if you've met them? You London folk all know each other, I dare say."

"That's most kind of you, but—"

"Now, don't say you have another engagement." Lady Thwaite had an air of suppressed triumph. "The Millways are coming, and there will be Mr. Haining too. And really, I can't *imagine* what else you could be doing."

Crane could think of a number of occupations that would give him more pleasure, even in Piper. "I'm not engaged, as such, but I'm extremely busy. Matters are in something of a tangle here. I really can't spare the time for social events, I'm afraid. Thank you anyway." He rose as he spoke.

"But you must come." Lady Thwaite stood too and took hold of Crane's hand. "Listen to me. You can't refuse to meet your neighbours and you really mustn't decline. Come tonight, at seven, or you will offend us all and you don't want to do that."

"I—"

"Listen to me. You don't want to refuse at all, dear Lord Crane. You know you must come. You have to meet Helen again. You like Helen so much, she's so sweet and pretty. Such a lovely girl. So suitable, so eligible. You must come."

Crane sighed internally, realising he would have to go. "Very well, then, thank you. But I've a guest with me here."

"Bring him along!" said Sir James boisterously, getting in before his wife could speak. "The more the merrier."

"I've no idea if he has dining clothes—"

"Oh, don't bother about that!" said Sir James merrily. "We're not sticklers, are we, my dear?"

Lady Thwaite patted Crane on the arm with a victorious smirk. "Of course not. And you must come, dear Lord Crane, you really, really must."

Crane returned to his work for ten minutes or so after the Thwaites had left, cursing himself for giving in to a pointless social obligation, and wondering what the devil Stephen could wear to any kind of dinner. The man was barely presentable as it was. He caught himself reflecting that his own amber cufflinks would match Stephen's eyes, the blend of warm brown and glowing gold, and wondered why he'd had that thought, because Stephen's eyes were a drab clay colour...

He put his pen down.

He *knew* the man's eyes were golden, changeable, intense. He'd watched them long enough. But he also knew they were dull and unattractive, because...

Because Stephen had told him so?

Crane made himself go over and over the last night, memories swimming to the surface as he concentrated. The cold rough stone. Stephen on his knees. Warm breath and soft lips against his hand.

He knew it had all happened. But part of his mind was insisting it hadn't—because Stephen had made him think it hadn't. Because Stephen had gone into his mind, and practiced on his thoughts.

Stephen, the shaman he trusted to protect him, the man he had started thinking of as his friend.

Crane stared unseeingly at the surface of the desk, face tightening as he thought it over. When he was sure he was right, he got up, walked out of the room to the library and knocked on the door in a restrained, calm, steady fashion for about five minutes without stopping, until several rather confused-looking servants had gathered round him and his knuckles were getting sore.

Finally Stephen opened the door a crack and gave him a look of exasperation. Crane responded with a bland smile, and kicked the door open so hard that the other man had to leap back to avoid being hit.

Stephen had barely slept the previous night. He had compounded that shameless performance in the garden with a disgraceful abuse of his powers: he had tortured himself for half the night with reproaches and the other half with images of what might have been, painfully aware of Crane oblivious and asleep in the next room. He had been scarcely able to meet Crane's eyes at breakfast for anger at himself, and he had spent the morning getting increasingly frustrated at the maddening difficulty of casting in this ridiculous, hateful house. It had taken him hours to get into a state of focus that meant he could force the meagre ether to do his bidding, and the knocking that broke his concentration was almost as unwelcome as the results he was seeing, or the heavy oak door that came within two inches of breaking his nose.

"What the *devil*?" he demanded as Crane strode in and back-heeled the door shut with a slam.

"I," said Crane sweetly, "have just accepted a dinner invitation for us both. Tonight."

"You've done what? Why?"

"That's what I'd like to know," said Crane. He stalked forward. Stephen dropped back a pace. "I was happily refusing the importunities of a pair of dullards, when quite suddenly I found myself realising that I was being terribly rude and it was absolutely necessary that I should attend this tedious social engagement. Much as, in the past weeks, I have found myself thinking that I was a worthless piece of human waste who ought to kill myself."

"Oh! You think—"

"*Much as*," Crane went on over him, taking another step forward so that Stephen was backed up against the desk, "last night, just after you revealed yourself as the world's best card-sharper and faced down a bloody *ghost*, I found myself thinking that you're really a very dull little man that I don't want to pay any attention to. Isn't that odd?"

Stephen froze. Crane glared at him, ugly with rage, clenching his fists. "You damned little swine, how dare you play the fool with my mind?"

He pushed Stephen backwards. The smaller man squirmed sideways. "Not the desk, don't knock the desk!" he yelped. "I've spent all morning doing that—"

"The hell with the desk," said Crane, shoving it hard. There was a sad tinkling clatter as a tangle of something metallic collapsed, and Stephen gave a pained cry of protest, which Crane ignored, reaching for him again. Stephen ducked under his arm and sidestepped. Crane grabbed him by the shoulders, walked him back two paces and slammed him against a bookshelf.

"Ow."

Crane stared down. Stephen knew he had a slight flush in his cheeks, but he met Crane's eyes directly.

"Well?" demanded Crane.

"Well, you're right, of course."

"*Why?*"

Stephen looked at him steadily, chin tilted slightly up, refusing to drop his eyes. "It's safer."

"For whom?"

"Me. Can you let me go, please, I've got some sort of atlas in my back."

Crane shifted his hands from Stephen's shoulders to the shelves behind, but didn't otherwise move, so that Stephen was still trapped by his body and outstretched arms.

"That was neither an explanation, nor an apology," Crane said. "I want both. What did you do to me?"

"I put fluence on you. Influence. To lead your thoughts in the direction I wanted them to go."

"Why?" asked Crane again.

"If I wanted to discuss it, I wouldn't have used fluence in the first place. You know, I'm used to people being taller than me, and I really don't find it as intimidating as you may imagine, so you may as well step back."

Crane leaned forward and down instead, eyes snapping with fury. "Will you be more intimidated when I wring your neck, you little sod?"

Stephen reached up and put a finger on Crane's throat. "Listen to me. Step back two paces, calmly."

Crane stepped back. Stephen rolled his narrow shoulders and took a breath, counting mentally. When he reached six, he saw the rage ignite in Crane's face and rapidly moved away from the wall.

"You fucking little shit!"

Crane lunged. Stephen ducked, jinked sideways and retreated in earnest as Crane went for him, far faster than he'd anticipated. He skipped backwards and found Crane had backed him against the desk again. The taller man grabbed him, astonishingly hard, and threw him backwards, so that the breath burst out of him, and before he could move, Crane was over him, pinning him down.

Stephen's back was on the desk, and his feet didn't reach the floor. Crane leaned on him, bodies pressed close, pinioning his wrists above his head, face dark with anger.

It occurred to Stephen Day that he had just made a fairly spectacular misjudgement.

"I apologise for that." He spoke as calmly as possible, trying to ignore the pressure of Crane's body against his. "It was in the way of an experiment, to see how fast you'd shake it. You're developing surprisingly rapid resistance to fluence."

"Perhaps that's because people keep doing it to me," said Crane through his teeth.

Stephen's brows drew together slightly. "I think you may be right, at that. How—"

"No," said Crane. "I'm asking the questions."

He was pressing down painfully on Stephen's wrists, taut body just over Stephen's, hard and intent and all too close to the night's imaginings. Stephen swallowed, cursing the betraying rush of blood, wishing he dared shift position.

"This is quite uncomfortable."

"Good. I remembered what happened last night."

"Nothing happened," said Stephen instantly, defensively.

"Yes, it did. There was a ghost."

"Oh—well, yes—"

"But that wasn't what you had in mind, was it?"

Stephen bit his lip. *Control this.* "Why don't you tell me what you think happened last night?"

Crane's lips drew back in a snarl. "What I *think* is that I was about to have you right there in the garden. I *think* you were about two minutes from being flat on your back in the grass."

Stephen felt the blood recede from his face. *Brilliant, Steph, well played.*

"And…" Crane shifted his leg up so that it rubbed against Stephen's painfully tight groin, ridding him of the admittedly faint hope that Crane hadn't noticed his arousal. "I *think* you're two minutes from the same thing right now."

"Oh God," said Stephen involuntarily. He couldn't tell if Crane meant it, or what he meant. A dizzying pulse of excitement was making it difficult to think. Crane's body was hard against him, and he could feel the larger man's cock, pressing against his stomach. "Listen—"

"Shut the fuck up!" It was a shout, but Crane's voice moved immediately to a savage purr. "I want to make you pay for that right now, you manipulative little bastard. I want to make you pay, and you know it, and…" His mouth curled, and he shoved his thigh cruelly against Stephen's erection again. "And you like it. In fact, I suspect there's nothing you'd like better. Is there?"

Stephen couldn't speak, couldn't move.

"Well?"

Stephen licked his lips. "What do you want me to say?" His voice sounded breathy in his own ears.

"Tell me why you did that to me last night. And don't lie to me. I know what you wanted, what you want. So why did you do it?"

He did not want to answer that. "I— It was—"

"You wanted me to fuck you, didn't you?"

Stephen shut his eyes. "Briefly."

Crane lowered his head so his mouth was right on Stephen's ear, voice vibrating, teeth and tongue touching the sensitive flesh. "When I fuck you, Mr. Day, it will not be briefly. It will be long and hard and extremely thorough. I'm going to take *pains* with you."

Stephen whimpered, helpless to stop himself, tilting his hips so his cock rubbed against Crane's body. Crane thrust back hard, once, grinned mirthlessly at Stephen's gasp, and leaned back with a look of victory in his eyes.

"Let's consider this in the nature of reparations." He shifted one hand so that it pinioned both of Stephen's wrists and moved his free hand to his belt.

There was a cruel twist to his mouth, and the fleeting, hateful resemblance hit Stephen with shocking vividness. A sudden flare of all-consuming rage leapt in his mind, obliterating his arousal. "God damn it, your father ruined mine, your brother assaulted my mother, and you think I'm going to let a Vaudrey have me, here? Get off me!"

He shoved, hard, putting power behind it, but Crane had already let go of his wrists and recoiled from the desk as though

Stephen was a poisonous thing. He strode to the window and stood, gripping the frame, staring out.

Stephen sat up awkwardly and took a very deep breath. He leaned forward and put his face in his hands.

There was a long, unpleasant silence.

"I didn't think of that." Crane didn't look round when he finally spoke. "I don't think of myself as part of my family, you see. I didn't think you did. I thought you didn't. Of course you do."

"I don't," Stephen said. "If I did, I wouldn't have got into that situation in the first place. It was just—then..."

You looked like Hector. Looking at Crane's rigid back, he couldn't have said the words at gunpoint.

"I panicked," he went on. "That's all I can say. I panicked last night, and I abused my powers and your mind to get myself out of an awkward situation. You've every right to be angry."

"Angry, yes." Crane still didn't look round. "Not to behave like my brother."

"Oh, please," Stephen said wearily. "We both know that's not true."

Crane turned at last, face tight. "Horse shit. I'm twice your size."

"Yes, and I'm a practitioner, and you have no concept of what I can do," Stephen snapped. "Don't dare assume I can't defend myself."

"So why didn't you?" Crane retorted instantly.

"Because I didn't want to. As you so astutely observed. I think you've probably humiliated me enough for now, don't you?"

He rested his head on his hand, legs dangling over the side of the desk, trying to make his body stop clamouring for sex or violence or both. He could feel Crane watching him, and the anger draining out of the room.

"Alright," Crane said finally. "You abused my mind. I had every intention of abusing you right back. The only possible conclusion is that we're a pair of bastards."

Stephen's lips twitched.

"Did I hurt you?"

"Only my pride. And my wrists. And my entire morning's work."

"I'm sorry."

"Forget it." Stephen sighed. "Lord Crane—"

"Crane, for God's sake. I can't stand the title, it sounds like my father's in the room."

"Crane," said Stephen, tasting the unadorned name. "I apologise for last night. And I give you my word I won't do that again, fluence you. It's really not how I generally conduct myself."

"Nor I. You hit a sore point. I suppose this whole business is a lot of sore points strung together for you."

"It isn't terribly easy," Stephen agreed.

Their eyes met for a moment. Crane gave him a crooked smile. "What do you want to do about this?"

"My job. That's all. Without complicating things."

"You don't feel things are getting complicated all by themselves?"

"No," Stephen said. "I think it's mostly me and I think I should stop it."

"It's not mostly you. But... Alright. I won't resume this subject unless you do. If you don't, I'll respect that. But if you do, Mr. Day, I will take it you've made your mind up. Your choice."

Stephen didn't want it to be his choice. He wanted to be an extremely long way away from Crane, so that choice didn't come in to it. But he nodded anyway, because there wasn't much else to do, and they stood in awkward silence for a moment.

"Work," Stephen said finally. "Can we go back to this dinner invitation?"

"The— Oh, yes, that. Right. What happened was that Sir James and Lady Thwaite, of Huckerby Place, made me think I had to accept a dinner invitation. That sounds ridiculous."

"When you accepted this invitation, did either of them touch you?"

Crane frowned. "I have an idea Lady Thwaite took my hand."

"May I?"

Crane extended his hand. Stephen took it—*professional, Stephen*—turned it over thoughtfully, brought his face down and sniffed deeply, running his nose just above Crane's skin.

"What in God's name are you doing?"

"Witch-smelling." Stephen sniffed again. "There's definitely something there. Fluence. Not me."

"So this fluence requires physical contact, does it?"

"Skin contact. Have you any idea what Lady Thwaite was saying?"

"I'm not sure." Crane frowned. "I can't seem to remember the words. I just know that she changed the way I thought. As you did, as the Judas jack did."

"Why on earth would she fluence you just to accept an invitation?"

"No idea. But I don't think it's the first time she's done it."

"Really." Stephen felt the familiar prickle along his spine, the hackles of the hunting dog. "Is anything striking you as odd about your previous relations with her?"

"That I have any," Crane said. "I've been ignoring cards and refusing invitations since I got back, but I found myself visiting the Thwaites on each of my previous visits down here. I may add, if I wanted to get to know any of my neighbours, it wouldn't be them."

"Does your presence lend social cachet?"

Crane shrugged. "Well, I'm the new Earl Crane, but on the other hand, I'm the old Lucien Vaudrey. And they're an established country family anyway. I'd scarcely think it was worth the effort, certainly not three times over. There was nobody else there the second time, in fact, just the Thwaites and their daughter."

"Ah," said Stephen. "Their unmarried daughter, is that?"

"They've only the one. Midtwenties, unmarried, very pretty, very charming—what?"

Stephen kept his face inexpressive, biting back an inappropriate urge to laugh. "Out of curiosity, have you been having any thoughts of matrimony, at all?"

"Well, it's crossed my mind. For obvious reasons, I'm not inclined to marry, but there's the succession...which...which I don't give a damn about..." Crane's voice tailed off, then he exploded, "That fucking harpy!" He stalked a few paces, spine stiff with anger. "Do you seriously think I was being entrapped into marriage by magic?"

"It's possible," Stephen said. "Fluence wouldn't do it alone, but if Miss Thwaite is pretty and charming, it could certainly pave the way. You're the last Vaudrey, you're in search of a wife and an heir—"

"I'm not. I am *not*."

"You might be expected to be," said Stephen patiently. "Wealthy neighbours, lovely daughter, good family. You might well be led to feel she'd do as well as another."

The darkness was back behind Crane's eyes. "She is not charming. She's a thoroughly nasty, foul-tempered piece of work. I am not going to marry that ill-conditioned little shrew, and I will not be manipulated by that sour-faced bitch her mother!"

"No, you won't," Stephen said. "I'll put a stop to it."

"Do you think she'll listen to you?"

"I expect so. You said I was invited tonight?"

"We're not going," said Crane emphatically.

"I think we should. I need to see Lady Thwaite in action, if possible, make sure it *is* her. I won't let anyone assault your virtue," he added, and received a withering glare.

"*Tsaena.* Bloody woman. Oh dear God. Is she the jack's maker?"

"Not if she's also trying to marry you to her daughter, surely. But anyway, the jack came from around Nethercote, which is the opposite direction to Huckerby Place. I could show you the pinpointer, except you wrecked it."

Crane looked down at the chaos on the desk. A map was spread out on the faded green leather top. A couple of contorted needles lay by it, and a mess of twisted fragments of wood. There was a small pool of solid tin, the size of a fingernail, on the leather, a few pieces of broken needle stabbed randomly into the desk surface, some papers and a pen wiper. A tangle of needles lay like spillikins on the map.

"Sorry."

"I'd got the location, at least. It was a phenomenally difficult piece of work. Everything in here is flowing in the most peculiar way. But I did get Nethercote. Definitely."

Crane was looking closely at him. "Is that a problem?"

Stephen sighed. "My Aunt Annie lives just outside Nethercote."

"I see," said Crane. "No, I don't. So what? Unless she's like my Great-Aunt Lucie, in which case you have all my sympathy—"

"She's a witch."

"Just like Great-Aunt Lucie."

"No," Stephen said. "She's a *witch*."

"Oh. I see. Oh, the devil—you don't think—"

"The jack? I can't think so," Stephen said. "Father's been dead twelve years, why would she do it now? And she's always been a stickler. It's just, I only know of one other practitioner in Nethercote and I find it hard to believe it was her either—Mrs. Parrott, her name is, a respected craftswoman. But there may well be someone else. This is the devil of an area for the craft, you know, so much power. I can't think why this house is so bad."

"So what do we do?"

"Have some lunch, go to Nethercote, talk to Mrs. Parrott and see if she can lead us to the maker. And hope to God my aunt doesn't turn up."

Chapter Ten

Nethercote barely earned the name of hamlet. There was a stagnant willow-hung pond around which stood a tiny, ancient, grey stone church, lit by the afternoon sun, and five cottages, two badly tumbledown.

Merrick tied the reins of the dogcart as Stephen and Crane looked around.

"Is this it?" Crane asked.

"This is Nethercote, yes, my lord."

"God almighty. I want to go home."

"You give the word, I'll book the boat," said Merrick. "We could be drinking Shaoxing wine in, what, two months if you stopped mucking round here. What do we do now, sir?"

"Don't ask me," Crane said.

"I wasn't," said Merrick, with ineffable scorn.

Stephen was still surveying the area. A dusty, patchwork-clothed boy of about seven was staring at them from behind a heap of stones. Stephen beckoned him over, and he came reluctantly, pausing about twelve feet away.

"Hey," Stephen said, holding out a tuppenny bit. "Can you tell me where Mrs. Parrott lives?"

The boy stared, wide eyes fixed on the coin. He reached out a tentative hand, changed his mind and darted away.

"He's probably never seen anyone who wasn't his first cousin," Crane said.

Stephen shrugged and strolled over to a rickety house front with a few bits of broken woodwork in front of it. There was a faint, tuneless whistling from inside, the kind hissed through a gap in the teeth, and a brief outbreak of hammering.

"Hello?" he called. "Anyone in? Good afternoon," he added, as a skinny man in fustian emerged, scowling. "Sorry to trouble you. Can you tell me where I can find Mrs. Parrott?"

The man snorted. "Try the church?" he said. "Reckon you find her there." He looked as though he was about to continue, but stopped, mouth slightly open, eyes fixed on Crane. He blinked a couple of times and darted back into his dark workshop without a goodbye.

"Charming," Crane muttered.

"Well, if you must wear a suit costing more than this entire village, you can expect to be stared at," Stephen said.

"Nobody could level that accusation at you." Crane headed to the churchyard wall. The tiny building looked deserted, the roof as though it wasn't far from collapse. The iron-grey aged oak door was firmly closed.

"Could she be inside?" Stephen asked dubiously. He walked up to the ivy-grown lychgate and cocked his head sideways, examining it.

Crane went through the lychgate without waiting, brushing past Stephen, who didn't react, and strolled through the daisies and buttercups that grew in profusion over the lichened tombstones around the church. "I doubt it," he called over his shoulder. "My experience of the rural sense of humour—yes, here we are."

Stephen and Merrick joined him. The neat new gravestone had some withered daffodils left by it, and the inscription was clear.

"Edna Parrott, dearly departed," Stephen read. "Two months ago. Good God, Mrs. Parrott dead, I thought she'd live forever. Well, that's a nuisance. I'll need her replacement. I wonder if we can find someone to ask about that."

"Reckon so," said Merrick, in a tone that made the other two look round.

Heading across the dusty road towards them, with a determined air, was a band of people. The carpenter was marching next to a big, burly man dressed like a farm labourer and a thinner, worried man. Two women, one sharp-faced and heavily pregnant and one tall, older, in a dark-brown stuff gown, accompanied them. The boy lurked alongside.

"A deputation," Stephen said.

"A mob, I expect." Crane led the way out of the churchyard. The little gang headed his way, faces hard with anger. Crane raised his hands in a pacifying gesture and walked forward to meet them. Merrick hurried at his long-legged master's heels.

There was a susurrus of anger as Crane came up to the villagers.

"Good afternoon. I'm Crane."

"We know who you are," said the pregnant woman shrilly. "What are you doing here?"

"My lord," mumbled the thin man with an apologetic dip of the head.

"No lord of ours." The pregnant woman spoke to a mumble of approval. "And no Vaudrey got any right to set foot in this place any more. We don't want you here."

"We won't be here long," said Crane. "We came in search of Mrs. Edna Parrott."

The pregnant woman gaped for a second, then screeched, "Pig! Filthy pig!" and rushed at Crane, hands outstretched like claws, nails out for his eyes. Crane sidestepped; Merrick caught her round the hips and spun her away. The big labourer gave a roar of rage and pulled back a ham-like hand, ready to land a sledgehammer punch on Crane, who skipped back a few steps, hands spread wide and conciliating, saying loudly, "*Don't* do that. Do *not*."

"I'll knock your damned head off for you," growled the big man, lumbering forward. Crane sidestepped again.

"Please don't. I never learned to fight like a gentleman. It would be ugly. And this lady is endangering herself."

The pregnant woman was thrashing and screaming curses, but unable to break Merrick's grip. Crane glanced at the other woman, who had her arms folded. "Madam, could you persuade this lady not to overexert herself?"

"If she wants to scratch your eyes out before Henry packs you on your way, *I* don't care."

The labourer moved towards Crane again, fists up, and Stephen flung a gloveless hand up so that it smacked against the labourer's meaty fist and said, "Stop."

There was a second's silence as the big man froze in place. Stephen's arm was stretched high to reach the other's hand, and he was dwarfed by the labourer's bulk, but there was no question at all who dominated the scene.

"Listen to me. Stop." Stephen moved his hand down and took the big man's arm with it in an unnervingly fluent way. "You don't want to hit Lord Crane. You don't want to be involved. You want to take your wife home. No fighting. Go home."

"Liza." The big man turned obediently away. "Come on, now. Let's us go."

The pregnant woman gaped at him and appealed to the woman in brown. "Marjorie!"

"Go home, madam," Stephen said. "Henry, listen to me, take your wife home now."

"Marjorie—" The pregnant woman fell silent as the big man put a heavy arm on her shoulders. Merrick let her go, exchanging a quick glance with Crane.

The woman in brown was thin-lipped, glaring between Stephen and Crane. "Go on, Liza. Think of the baby. I'll deal with this."

"And the rest of the spectators," Stephen said. "You, you and you. Off you all go. Now, please."

"You don't give the orders here," said the woman called Marjorie.

Stephen flicked a glance at her. "Yes, I do."

Merrick and Crane watched in silence as the small, bewildered group trailed away. The woman in brown stood alone, staring resentfully at Stephen.

"Right," she said. "You're here for Edna Parrott, are you? Well, she's dead. So if *he's* here to finish the job his brother started—"

"What's your grievance against Lord Crane?"

"He's a damned Vaudrey!"

"*Lucien* Vaudrey," Crane put in. "Not Hector, not Quentin. Lucien. The one who's been five thousand miles away for twenty years. I have no idea what my father or brother did to you, or to this place. Perhaps you could tell me."

"I don't have to tell you anything." The woman's arms were tightly folded. "Just get out and take your dogs with you. You've no right to be here."

"Wrong," said Stephen. "I am a justiciar, and I am here on a matter of dark practice and murder. I am requesting you to speak to me now."

"And what if I don't?" said the woman through stiff lips.

"Then it will stop being a request."

The woman's face was set like stone. She stared at Stephen, eyes dark, and Crane suddenly realised her pupils were dilating.

"Don't be silly," Stephen said, with a touch of impatience.

"This is my place," she said, low and angry. "I have rights."

"And you have duties," said Stephen. "What's your name?"

"Bell. Marjorie Bell. I'm Gammer's granddaughter."

"I'm Justiciar Stephen Day. This is Lord Crane, that's Mr. Merrick. Now—"

"*Stephen Day?*"

There was just a hint of a pause before Stephen nodded.

"Nan Talbot's nephew Stephen?"

"Yes."

Her mouth dropped open, a picture of incredulous contempt. "Allan Day's son? Helping the Vaudreys? Your father must be turning in his grave."

"My father knew his duty," said Stephen stonily. "He did his job, and I am doing mine. Starting now, Miss Bell."

"Does Nan Talbot know you're working for *that*?" She jerked her head at Crane.

"*Now.*"

Miss Bell went a deeper red. She spun and led the way with angry nervous steps to one of the cottages. The boy ran up to her as she walked; she said something quietly to him and he hurried away.

The cottage looked neglected, the plants outside withered and dead, and the door stood open.

They filed inside, Merrick leaning against the door to discourage eavesdropping. It was dark and dusty with an accretion of spider webs in the corners, smelling of dead fires and some acrid scent Crane couldn't place. The air felt withered and old and greasy. Crane, who was starting to recognise some things, darted a look at Stephen and saw him rubbing his fingertips together like a pastry cook at work.

Miss Bell said, "This was Gammer's cottage. What do you want here?"

Stephen ignored her. He was walking around, touching walls, running his hands over furniture, testing the air. He stopped for several minutes in the tiny kitchen, hands planted on the table, quivering slightly, returned to an old oak dresser, pulled out just one drawer, which seemed to be full of bits of fur and leather, and rummaged through it.

It took about ten minutes, and in that time nobody spoke. Miss Bell adopted a neutral expression and seated herself, on an uncomfortable straight-backed chair instead of the rocking chair that stood in the corner. She sat, looking into nothing, as though she would be happy to stay there all day. Crane leaned his shoulders against the slightly damp plaster of a wall and watched Stephen's intent face and searching, restless hands.

Finally Stephen looked round.

"It was her. Gammer Parrott. The Judas jack was made in the kitchen. The ivy wood came from the lychgate. It killed two men, nearly killed a third. Tell me, when did she turn warlock?"

"She did not turn," said Miss Bell fiercely.

"I took that jack apart. It wasn't a novice effort. She'd done it before."

"She never did! She didn't turn!"

Stephen looked at her assessingly. "Why did she do it?"

Her lips were pressed together tightly. "What's the good in me talking to you?"

"Miss Bell, if I'd already made my mind up, you would already know about it," Stephen said. "And Lord Crane spent two months under a vicious jack. He's got a right to know why."

"He's got no rights. None."

Stephen's voice was measured, implacable. "You will answer me."

She gave him a long, considering look. There was another lengthy silence. Finally she sniffed and began, speaking to Stephen only, without a glance at Crane.

"Gammer Parrott had two daughters, my ma and my Auntie Effie. And Effie had two daughters too. Liza Trent, you saw her outside, and Ruthie, Ruth Baker. Ruthie was the child of Effie's age, she was forty-six, and Baker long dead. Too old for childbearing. She died in her labour. She never named the father, but we all saw Ruthie's looks.

"She was a pretty girl, lively, but she didn't have enough brain to know which way the sun rises. And when she was fifteen, Hector Vaudrey got her with child." She looked at Crane for the first time. "Maybe he didn't know she was his daughter, maybe he didn't care if she was. Maybe it was what he wanted from her."

Crane shut his eyes and leaned his head back against the plaster wall.

"Was it by force?" Stephen asked.

"No need," said Miss Bell shortly. "He told Ruthie he'd marry her. She wasn't a clever girl."

"Clearly." Crane's voice was cold, eyes still shut. "Let me guess the next part. She finds out she's expecting, goes to Hector demanding the promised marriage, he laughs in her face, she goes to my father for justice and he sends her to the Magdalen. Yes?"

Miss Bell shook her head. "She didn't go to the Earl. What would be the point? Nobody went to him for justice against Hector Vaudrey, because nobody got it. No. Ruthie told Gammer about the baby. Gammer was angry. She'd have come round, she loved Ruthie, but things were said. And then...Ruthie learned who her father was."

"How?" asked Stephen and Crane simultaneously.

Miss Bell's jaw jutted. "I could never find that out."

"And what did Ruthie do when she knew?"

"She hanged herself. She was six months gone."

Stephen nodded slowly. "When?"

"Candlemas two years since."

Crane rubbed his fingers over the bridge of his nose. Miss Bell was watching him.

"Gammer went to the Earl," she said. "Told him what Hector Vaudrey had done. He ordered her to be whipped for slander."

Crane winced. Stephen nodded again. "And Mrs. Parrott made the jack after that. Alone?"

"I'd have helped her," said Miss Bell defiantly. "I would. But she didn't ask for my help."

Stephen looked round. "Lord Crane, any comment?"

"What on earth is there to say?" Crane said. He had a hand over his face. "His *daughter*."

"Mrs. Parrott killed him for it."

"Good," said Crane with some force.

"And your father for abetting him. Slowly and painfully. Does that bother you?"

"No."

"Right," Stephen said. "Moving on—"

"Moving on?" said Miss Bell incredulously.

"Moving on," Stephen repeated. "Lucien Vaudrey returns from twenty years on the other side of the world and promptly finds himself enslaved to a Judas jack, left there long after the guilty men were rotting in the ground. Tell me about that, Miss Bell. Tell me why you and Mrs. Parrott decided to kill an innocent man."

"I'll tell you why," said Miss Bell loudly. "Because we didn't want another Vaudrey just like the last two. It's easy enough to come down from London with your justice, but we had Hector Vaudrey's ways for thirty years, and we've all heard about *him*." She gestured at Crane with her chin. "Do you blame us?"

"Yes," said Stephen. "I do. Lucien Vaudrey was not responsible for his father's and brother's acts. You know that."

"Hector Vaudrey raped—"

"I know what Hector Vaudrey did. He'd been doing it for years. If you and Gammer Parrott had done something about it before, Ruthie would be alive now."

Crane sucked in an audible breath. Miss Bell gasped. "How *dare* you!"

"Other families suffered at Hector Vaudrey's hands. You did nothing until he hurt *your* family, and then tried to kill a man who had nothing to do with your wrongs. I don't call that justice."

Miss Bell's mouth worked. "And this *is* justice?" she managed. "Come in here when they're dead and tell us what we did wrong? What did *you* do about Hector Vaudrey?"

"Nothing," Stephen said coldly. "Lychdale is sufficiently stocked with lawyers, practitioners, guns, sharp-edged farming implements, poisons and kindling to get rid of a hundred Hectors. The only possible conclusion is that you all liked having him around."

Crane put a hand over his face at that; Merrick gave a little whistle. Miss Bell was scarlet, with spots of white on her cheeks and the sides of her nose.

"Now," Stephen went on. "Can you explain why leaving the jack for Lucien Vaudrey was other than murder? Can you justify killing a man you'd never even seen for the acts of his brother?"

"I can," said Crane, over Miss Bell's speechlessness.

"I beg your pardon?"

"I said, I can give you a reason. My father could tolerate Hector but he couldn't countenance me. Everyone expects me to be at least as bad as my brother. You did yourself."

"I didn't try to kill you."

"You've a heart of gold," Crane said sardonically. "In Mrs. Parrott or Miss Bell's shoes, I would have done precisely the same thing: kill them all and let God sort them out." Miss Bell made a slight gasp of protest; Crane went on. "Hector and my father brought their ends on themselves. And I am happy to regard the attempt on my life as an understandable precaution, as long as I know it will not be repeated." Crane looked over Stephen's head at Miss Bell. "I am not like my brother, madam. If you will accept that, this can end now."

"I'm the justiciar here," said Stephen with unusual belligerence. "*I* will tell *you* when this ends."

110

Crane's chin went up instinctively. "And I'm the lord here, and you're on my land."

"Your land, and your laws, is it?"

"I choose whether to prosecute a crime against myself," said Crane. "You've heard my wishes, Mr. Day. If this lady will drop the matter, so will I, and so will you. Madam?"

She opened her mouth, closed it, and glanced over at Stephen, whose face was stony.

"You're saying you're not like Hector Vaudrey," she said slowly. "But you're asking me to take a Vaudrey's word for it."

"Not really. And I suspect you know that. Talk to Mrs. Mitching up at Piper. Talk to Graham, if you like. Thank you, Merrick," he added, at the snort from the door. "I am far from spotless, but even Graham won't be able to tell you that I behave like my brother."

She walked over to Crane and looked up at him. "Give me your hand."

Crane extended it, gazing at her levelly. She looked down at it, turning it over and back.

"I'll accept what you say," she said at last. "For now. But you needn't expect any mercy if it turns out I shouldn't."

"No," said Stephen. "You will not act on this man in any way, under any circumstances, ever."

"*Mr. Day—*"

"No," said Stephen again, this time to Crane. "I'll respect your wishes, but there is a caveat and it is this: You have lost the benefit of the doubt, Miss Bell. If you believe action is needed against Lord Crane, you may call on me, but you will not take it yourself or cause it to be taken by others. If you move against this man by any means, direct or indirect, practice or material, you will be judged, and not kindly. Understood?"

She gave a stiff, resentful nod.

"I am going to draw a line under this business, at Lord Crane's request. But you are charged to spread the word that my attention is on the matter. If *anyone* harms Lord Crane, I will be back, and I will be unhappy, and I will spread that unhappiness far and wide and deep before I've done. Make that known round Lychdale. Are we clear, Miss Bell?"

Miss Bell's face was tight and mask-like. "Yes," she rapped.

"Good. Lord Crane, is there anything else?"

"Does Ruthie have a gravestone?" asked Crane.

The words fell into blank silence.

"Why?" asked Stephen cautiously.

"Suicide."

"No," said Miss Bell. "She don't. An unmarked grave outside the church wall is what Vicar gave her."

"Which church, the one here?"

"Saint Sulpice, in Fulford. He wouldn't let her lie here."

"Which vicar?"

"Mr. Haining."

"Does it matter to Mrs. Trent?"

"Yes," said Miss Bell. "It does."

Crane nodded. "I'll speak to him."

She snorted. "We spoke to him. New churchwarden tried and tried. Went and begged Vicar, for Gammer's sake. Back and forth, he went. Vicar wouldn't hear it. Self-murdered is outside the Church, he said, and that's all there is."

"Well, we shall see," Crane said. "Thank you. Good day, madam. Let's go."

Chapter Eleven

They left the unhappy little cottage, emerged into the bright, clean sunshine, and took two steps in the direction of the carriage before the cry cut through the air.

"Stephen!"

"Oh *God*," said Stephen.

All four turned to see a short, fat woman marching up. Her bonnet was slightly askew, and her face was red with exertion and anger.

"Stephen Day! What's this I hear?"

"I'm working, Aunt," Stephen said quellingly, to no effect.

"Working for the Vaudreys?"

"No, *working*. At my profession."

"There is no justice that you can bring to this," said Mrs. Talbot through her teeth. "Have you gone mad? Your father—"

"My father has nothing to do with this," Stephen snapped. "And nor do you, Aunt."

She took a deep breath, swelling. "When I hear of my own nephew grovelling to the Vaudreys—"

"Oh, for God's sake," said Crane.

"*You*," began Mrs. Talbot with loathing.

"Nan..." Miss Bell interrupted, and there was a clamour of voices.

"I will not—"

"Listen, please—"

"This ridiculous business—"

"Everybody be quiet," said Stephen, in a normal speaking voice that managed to deaden the sound of all the rest. "Aunt, if you want to speak to me, we will do it in private. Lord Crane, wait for me please."

He went back into the cottage without waiting for answers or permission. Annie Talbot gave Crane a long, nasty look before following her nephew in. The door slammed.

Crane let rip a sentence in Shanghainese that made his henchman's eyebrows shoot up, and stalked away towards the graveyard. Merrick didn't follow. As Miss Bell, hesitating, started to turn away, he touched her arm. "Got a moment, ma'am?"

"What is it?"

"D'you know who I am?"

Miss Bell frowned. "You? You're Lord Crane's servant, ain't you?"

"I'm Frank Merrick." Miss Bell's puzzled expression didn't change, so he added, "Twenty years ago I was up here, courting Amy Pessell. If you're from round this way, you might remember about that. She lived on a farm just a mile or so down the road."

Her face changed, slowly, two decades of memory shifting.

"*You* were Amy Pessell's beau?"

"That's right."

"The man who knocked Hector Vaudrey's teeth out," said Miss Bell. "That was you?"

"*One* tooth," Merrick said. "That's all I got, then he gave me a hell of a drubbing. Then I got a flogging, after. *Then* Amy stood up in front of the old lord in court and says it's all lies and Hector never touched her—"

"She had a big family," Miss Bell said. "No father. She couldn't take the risk of crossing him."

"I know. So the old lord gives me a choice, right? Ten years hard for grievous assault *or*, he says, I can take a post as manservant to his rotten younger son what he's sending to China. Seventeen years old and bad to the bone. Needs a keeper. Right? And I say yes to that, because there's not a lot else for me except breaking rocks. And then, day before we go, I get a message from one of his men, and he says, if Lucien Vaudrey happens to fall overboard, no need to worry anyone'll blame me for it, and I can just disappear in Shanghai, no questions asked. Right?"

Miss Bell straightened her back. "His *father* said that?"

"It came from him. Yeah. And I think, well, the old lord wants Hector alive and Lucien dead. So Lucien must be something special, one way or the other. And I think, I got the whole voyage to China. I'll just see what kind of bloke he is before I shove him over the side." He nodded slowly, eyes remote with the memory. "And he's a snotty, arrogant little so-and-so who needs keeping on a leash till he grows up, but what I can see pretty quick is, he ain't Hector. So I think, I got nothing better to do, let's see where this goes. Right?"

"Right," said Miss Bell, hypnotised.

"Twenty years ago, that was. We started poor as hell. You would not believe how poor you can be in the slums of Shanghai. Didn't think we'd live through the first winter. But he never let me down. He got me through smallpox, and made a shaman, that's one of your lot, take a curse off of me, and that cost him. I smuggled him two hundred miles in a silk caravan to get him away from a warlord, and you don't want to know about *that*, never seen a carry-on like it. Twenty years, Miss Bell. I know that bloke inside out, good and bad. You lot down here don't have a clue."

"Well." Miss Bell was nonplussed.

"Took me five days on that ship to make sure of him. Mr. Day got his measure in an hour, if you ask me. And if ever a man had a right to hate the Vaudreys, Mr. Day does, but here he is, and fighting for my lord. Think on it, Miss Bell. We need a bit more thinking round here."

Miss Bell nodded, slowly. "I will."

"Good. Oh, and if you happen to be putting the word round like Mr. Day said, there's just another thing, if you got a chance to mention it as well?"

"What's that?"

"The next bloke takes a swing at my lord, I'm going to break both his arms," said Merrick. "And that'll give him trouble when he tries to pick his teeth up. That's all. Nice talking to you, ma'am."

He strolled over to Crane, who was propped against the lychgate. Miss Bell stared after him.

The cottage door opened. Stephen stalked out, stiff-legged and flushed. Mrs. Talbot followed, an ugly shade of angry crimson. Stephen went over to Crane without looking at anyone else.

"I dare say I've wasted your time," he snapped. "Jack's maker's dead, no need for me to protect you. I'm going to walk back."

"Do you want company?"

"No."

"Bad luck," said Crane amiably. "Merrick, can you drive back and see about Mr. Day's clothes for tonight?"

"Sir," said Merrick, flipping a cheery wave to Miss Bell, who was being buttonholed by Mrs. Talbot, as he got into the carriage.

Stephen set off at a rapid, angry pace down the leafy lane. Crane, whose extra height was mostly leg, kept up effortlessly with long, casual strides. It was very hot now, but the trees above shed welcome green shade, and magpies cawed and chirruped overhead. Their feet echoed slightly on the dry packed earth.

"Do you want to talk about it?" asked Crane.

"No."

They paced on for a moment.

"What's a justiciar?"

Stephen stared ahead. "You asked who enforces the laws surrounding practitioners. Justiciars do."

"And that's what you are."

"Yes."

"A secret policeman."

"It's not a secret."

"You didn't tell me."

"You're not a practitioner."

"Justiciar. Judge and jury?"

"If you like."

"So what's the penalty for killing someone with a Judas jack?"

"My job is to stop practitioners hurting people," said Stephen irritably. "I'd have stopped Gammer Parrott by whatever means necessary."

"You killed that warlock last winter," Crane observed.

"That was necessary."

"Judge, jury and executioner. What about Miss Bell? What's the maximum sentence for aiding and abetting murder?"

"It doesn't work like that. My job is to stop practitioners hurting people, and I do that however I have to."

"So you left Miss Bell disinclined to hurt me, by bullying and threatening her."

"If you want to put it like that," said Stephen, tight-lipped.

"Until you forced me and her into alliance. So I stood up for her, more or less proving she was wrong about me as I did so, and left her far better disposed towards me. I can feel my local reputation improving as we speak."

Stephen looked slowly round. Crane was grinning at him.

"Nicely played. Although when you're relying on my intervention, I'd rather you warn me in advance."

"I wasn't relying on anything. You had every right to demand redress, and I'd have supported that. Though I did think—hope—you might react as you did," Stephen added, slightly less stiffly. "It was...fair. And I'm glad of it. It's best for everyone to get her back on the straight and narrow."

"You've got that authority, to let her off?"

"Well, yes. Judge and jury."

"That's quite a responsibility."

"It's how your ancestor set it up," Stephen said. "The Magpie Lord founded the justiciary, he made the rules. Of course, *he* thought it would be an appointment of honour, not a job you give the misfits and the ones who can't pay for training."

"Not a popular job, then."

"No," Stephen said, with some emphasis. "Nobody likes the justiciary, sticking our noses into other people's business and telling our betters what to do. They can't stand us, right up till the moment they come up against someone stronger and more ruthless, and then they start clamouring for help and asking why we haven't done our jobs before." He kicked a stone into the white-blossomed hedgerow. "It's harder out here. In the cities, there's more danger but that means people understand more. Here, they just do what they like and treat the law like it's for other people."

"That attitude seems fairly common round here. I take it your aunt wasn't sympathetic."

"My aunt," said Stephen viciously. "Dear Aunt Annie. Apparently the fact that she's my father's sister gives her the right to decide what he'd have thought about any situation. Apparently, she knows the definition of justice better than I do. Apparently, any friend of hers, such as Gammer Parrott, is above the law. Or rather, it's impossible that dear Edna could have done a bad thing, therefore you must deserve the fate of the other Vaudreys regardless of evidence, and *therefore* there's only one reason for me to prevent you being murdered, and it has nothing to do with law or justice."

"And that is?"

"Well, let's see," Stephen said. "You're notorious for unspeakable vice. You've put me up in what ought to be your wife's bedroom. And Graham saw—*saw*—me commit an abominable act on you in the garden last night. So why don't you take a guess."

"Shit."

"I just want to know how exactly you've made sure everyone in Lychdale knows who you go to bed with," Stephen snapped. "You've only been in the country four months! Do you even stop to sleep? And between your abysmal reputation and a pair of damp trouser knees, Mr. Graham seems to have conjured up a story out of *Sins of the Cities of the Plain*, which allowed my aunt to accuse me of gross depravity with, more or less, my father's murderer."

"The bitch. Stephen—" Crane reached for him. He slithered sideways, away, and started walking again, a fast, angry march.

"It's what she wanted to hear," he went on. "It confirmed that she was quite right not to offer to house me when my father died, which she's been trying to justify for the last twelve years. It's entirely reasonable to abandon a homeless boy if he grows up to be a sodomite, especially with a Vaudrey involved. And I could hardly make a convincing denial of anything going on, could I?"

Crane put a hand through his hair. "I'm extremely sorry. I can probably make Graham recant—"

"It won't change her mind. I don't care anyway." Stephen halted abruptly. "Do you want me?"

"What?"

"Well, if I'm going to get talked about and screamed at and accused anyway... You can have me. Now. If you want."

"Out here?" Crane said incredulously. "Did they change the law without telling me?"

"There's nobody within a quarter of a mile."

"How can you possibly— Do you actually know that?"

"Yes," Stephen said. "For God's sake, do you want to do it or not?"

Crane grabbed the back of Stephen's head and tilted it back as he bent to force his mouth onto the smaller man's, hard, feeling him gasp. They stumbled to the side of the road and a few yards into the woods, lips awkwardly locked, and Crane pushed Stephen up against a tree. Stephen pulled at his shirt, and Crane grasped his wrists and shoved them back, either side of the tree trunk, pinioning him.

"I'm in charge," he said.

Stephen nodded, closing his eyes. His lips were reddened, but his face was rather pale.

Crane's hand slipped to Stephen's waist, unfastening buttons rapidly. Stephen was only semi-hard, but that changed rapidly as Crane went on his knees and took him in his mouth.

He licked and sucked with well-honed skill, using teeth and lips and tongue, and Stephen gripped his scalp desperately. Crane felt the prickle of those magical fingers as Stephen's arousal built. He brought him off quickly, not allowing him time to think, ignoring Stephen's warning groan and taking the magician's come in a salty rush to his mouth as Stephen jerked and spasmed against him, his electric fingertips sparking in Crane's hair.

Stephen slithered down the tree trunk and ended up sitting on the moss, mouth open, eyes shut.

"God," he said eventually. "You're very good at that."

Crane wiped his lips. "Practice makes perfect."

Stephen was still for another moment while his breathing returned to normal. He squared his shoulders slightly as he opened his eyes to meet Crane's. "How do you want me?"

"Uh-uh," said Crane. "Another time."

"What?"

KJ Charles

Crane leaned over and kissed him, deep but gentle now, letting Stephen feel his own salty sweetness on his tongue. At last he pulled away and rubbed Stephen's swollen lower lip with a light thumb. "When I have you, sweet boy, it will be because you want me to. Not against your better judgement, not in spite of my surname, and definitely not to annoy your aunt."

Stephen went red, but his voice was defiant. "Well, what was that, then?"

Crane shrugged. "You seemed tense."

Stephen gave an incredulous choke of laughter. His head whipped round. "Blast. Stay still."

His hands gave a quick jerk in the air, and he gripped Crane's arm, holding him steady, as two labourers strolled round the bend. They walked together, chatting idly, completely ignoring the two men sprawled together a few yards from the road, and disappeared up the lane. Crane stared after them until Stephen released his arm.

"*That* is useful," Crane said. "But, rather than using it again..." He got to his feet and pulled Stephen up, gently brushing his cropped hair for bark as Stephen rearranged his clothing.

"Look, Crane—Lucien—are you sure—"

"Yes," Crane said. "Don't worry, I'll take it out on you soon enough. Come on."

Chapter Twelve

Stephen Day contemplated himself in the spotty mirror with a sense of quietly impending doom. There were several reasons for this. The most trivial but most obvious was his clothing.

Merrick had done impressive work on his black suit, but there was no getting away from its age and cheapness: it was ill fitting; the black was rusty; and the elbows were worn, as always happened to his jackets because he always ended up propping himself on his elbows, occasionally in pools of various liquids. He'd definitely leaned in something in this one.

Usually the issue wouldn't have crossed his mind, but two days of Crane's sartorial perfection were getting to him. The man wore the best-cut suits Stephen had ever seen, of magnificent, understated quality, setting off the elegance of his long, rangy frame. Stephen couldn't imagine what he—or rather Merrick—did to his spotless linen to prevent the tattoos showing through like black stains across his chest. An image of Crane's muscular, magpie-etched torso flashed into his mind and he blinked it away, aware that he could have drawn a freehand map of the man's skin decoration based on those few seconds of fascinated attention a week ago.

Stephen was—had to be—realistic in his expectations. He didn't have either the height or the wealth to wear suits like

Crane, even if he'd cared enough about clothing to try, and he would never be physically impressive. Normally he was unconcerned by that. But normally he was a stone heavier and able to tap into the etheric flow. As it was, looking at the cheap suit hanging off his starveling frame, his thin, pale, worried face and horribly short hair, he was conscious of a wish he'd taken another month's convalescence as his doctor had attempted to order.

Well, too late to worry about that now. A larger concern was what he'd find at this dinner.

On its own, identifying and slapping down an abuse of power would be nothing, a daily chore. But someone fluencing Crane wasn't an isolated incident. It was part of a tangle of threads—the Judas jack, Hector's ghost, and the unpleasantly *wrong* atmosphere of Piper, which nagged at Stephen's instincts like a bad tooth.

It was of course possible that all these were separate matters, brought together by coincidence, but Stephen hadn't survived seven years as a justiciar by trusting to luck. So tonight he would watch, and wait, and work out how to unpick the knot of trouble around Crane.

This meant that he would be spending more time here, with him.

Considering the utter fool he had made of himself, for the second time that day, the walk home had been surprisingly tolerable. Crane had kept the conversation flowing: charming, fascinating, amusing. They had talked the whole way back and had reached Piper before Stephen's urge to curl up and die of self-inflicted embarrassment became unbearable. He had mumbled something about working in the library, suddenly desperate to hide away, and Crane...

Crane had said, "Then we will speak later," but as he spoke he had taken Stephen's chin in one hand and stroked that thumb over his lips, opening them with a firm, deliberate touch, so that Stephen found himself standing receptively, obediently, waiting.

That was all. It wasn't much. But they both knew that Crane could have him at the crook of one long, slender finger.

He could still feel those powerful hands on his shoulders, slamming him back against the bookshelves, throwing him onto the desk, holding him down. It had been humiliating, of course—his own arousal and Crane's bitingly accurate assessment of it. It had also been painfully, dangerously exciting, and Crane had known it, had identified Stephen's desires, and was quite evidently a match for them.

I'm in charge. I'll take it out on you.

Stephen didn't anticipate that Crane would let him off so easily next time, and he didn't want him to.

That didn't mean this was anything other than madness, of course.

How was your trip to the country, Steph? he imagined his partner asking.

Oh, I let a bored aristocrat use me as his new plaything, and now my Aunt Annie will never speak to me again. So-so, really.

A nice relaxing interlude, though, with a remarkably attractive man who'd normally never look twice at you, isn't that just what you needed?

Ah, well, you see, he replied to the imaginary Esther, *I could have just had a tumble in the grass, but I thought I'd wait and make sure of things. That he's a decent man. Fair-minded. The things that matter to me.*

He could almost see Esther rolling her eyes. He could never have had this conversation with her in reality, but he knew what she'd say all the same: *Well done, Steph. Why settle for a bit of simple pleasure when you could turn it into a hopeless passion for a man who could have anyone, and probably will?*

He sat on the four-poster bed, looking round at the faded wallpaper that splashed great pink peonies over the room, lit by the rapidly fading evening sun. He was extremely conscious that Crane was just beyond the connecting door, could hear him talking to Merrick in that extraordinary language that made it impossible even to guess at meaning. He thought they might be laughing.

When Stephen emerged from the house, the last of the golden light was turning cold but the evening air was like bathwater, a shock after the bone-chilling freeze of Piper.

Crane was lounging, looking predictably perfect in an impeccable dining suit. You wouldn't have thought he had a body like a sailor, or a mouth like one. Stephen gave a brief, convulsive shiver at the thought of that mouth.

Crane gave Stephen an up-and-down glance and waved him to the dogcart. There was no groom.

"Are you driving?" asked Stephen.

"Yes. So we can talk."

"Oh."

Crane flicked the reins and set the horses moving down the long avenue that led away from Piper. Stephen took a deep breath.

"I think I should apologise for that performance earlier. I made rather a fool of myself."

"If you think that was making a fool of yourself, you have a lot to learn," Crane said. "Some day you should bring a bottle of brandy down to the kitchen and get Merrick to tell you about the occasions I've really made a fool of myself. I promise you, the brandy will run out before the stories do." He shot Stephen a sideways glance. "Besides, it gave me the opportunity to put a smile on your face. I enjoyed that."

Stephen had no idea how to answer that. The horse trotted on. It was dark down the tree-lined lanes, and there was the occasional rustle of birds above and the harsh calls of nesting rooks and, probably, magpies.

"Tell me," Stephen said eventually. "Your local reputation...is it as widely spread as Aunt Annie suggested?"

"I dare say." Crane didn't sound concerned. "I was expelled from five schools, three of them for gross immorality. My father was happy to tell all and sundry that was why he was getting rid of me. And of course, there's no laws against it in China, so I lived as I chose, and word got back."

Stephen stared at him. "No laws?"

"No laws, no moral objections. Nobody cares. It's just one of the things people do. I'm sure my father didn't know *that* when he sent me there."

Stephen thought about that. "What about practice? Shamanism? Is that legal?"

"Yes, of course. Legal, acknowledged, shamans on every corner and advising the government— God, you look like a child outside a sweet shop."

"I feel like one," Stephen said. "No laws. You mean, like...normal?"

"Entirely normal." Crane shrugged. "I had a fairly intense fling with a youngish and rather lovely mandarin. He took me to the odd state banquet. Nobody raised an eyebrow. Except the

127

British contingent, the bacon-and-egg types. They didn't like it. I expect they wrote back to England in droves. Didn't bother me. I'd never planned to come back so I didn't care about my reputation in England—and, actually, after twenty years in a sane country, I don't care now. If I'm arrested Merrick will post bail and we'll get on the next ship back to civilisation."

"Can I come?" said Stephen, and blushed as the words left his mouth.

"By all means. The laws don't apply to you, though, surely?"

"Yes, of course they do. Well, they absolutely would if I was arrested and sentenced. Admittedly, I don't propose to let that happen, for witchcraft or anything else. But in theory, yes."

The horse trotted on.

"Tell me what's going to happen this evening," Crane said. "Will Lady Thwaite know you're a justiciar?"

"I don't expect so, unless she's heard from Miss Bell, but that seems unlikely. I'm not sure I'll act on her tonight, incidentally. I want to get a sense of what's going on here first. Would you mind letting her fluence you?"

"Yes, I bloody would!" said Crane with startling vehemence, jerking the reins. "I will *not* be played with like that." He was obviously forcing down anger as he went on, "I object to having my mind invaded. That is an absolute refusal. No."

Stephen frowned. "This is the sore point you mentioned, isn't it? What happened?"

Crane's mouth tightened. "Oh, we had a charming experience with one of your lot in China." He stared up into the trees, muscles twitching over his face. "In a word, Merrick rooked a shaman at dice, and the bastard put a curse on him that made him...imbecilic. Animal. It was disgusting. He drooled and gibbered. Smeared his shit on the walls and—*tsaena*. It
128

was grotesque. I thought he'd be like it forever." He jerked his head, shaking off the memory.

Stephen's hands were twitching compulsively with the urge to strike. On the occasions he thought of leaving his thankless, dangerous job, it was expressions like the one Crane was wearing now that made him keep on going. "How did it end?"

"I paid the shaman off. Everything we had, more or less. No choice. I tried to negotiate and he threatened to do the same thing to me. So I paid up, and he lifted the curse and went off smirking." Crane wiped a hand over his face. "I have plenty of bad memories but Merrick grinning in the corner like an ape is... No."

Stephen bit his lip. "And now I'm doubly ashamed of what I did last night. I won't let anyone touch you again. You have my word."

"Thank you."

"Er... That said, would you be able to tolerate an attempt if I promise it won't work?"

Crane shot him a look. "Why do you want me to?"

"Honestly, I want to find out what is going on around here. And the easiest way is to let them show us what they want."

Crane frowned. "Is this not just a rather silly woman abusing her powers?"

"Probably, yes. But what with the jack and the haunting, I'd like to be sure of that before I act."

"I see." Crane turned the horses through a gate. "I don't know. I can't promise to behave myself."

"Well, it's up to you," Stephen said. "You've heard my recommendation."

"I don't know. Oh, sod it. You're the expert. Whatever you want. What reason should we give for your presence?"

"Oh, legal business. Vague, dull legal business. Messuage, enfeoffment, conveyancing."

"Dull things. Right."

"I'm going to be fairly dull myself," Stephen said. "I plan to go unnoticed, as much as possible."

"As you wish. But it occurs to me that Graham will have spoken to the servants when the Thwaites visited. If they listen to servants' gossip…"

"Don't worry about it," Stephen said confidently. Away from Piper's malign influence, he could feel the stronger flow tingling through his blood. "Nobody is going to think of me in those terms."

"Well, I didn't like to say so, but that is a dreadful suit," Crane agreed, as he pulled up the horses outside the house. "You'd look much better out of it."

He climbed lithely down from the dogcart and handed the reins to the Thwaites' groom. Stephen muttered, "Swine," and followed, feeling a grin dawning irrepressibly on his face.

Chapter Thirteen

Huckerby Place was a far more opulent home than Piper, in that it was warm and welcoming and had been decorated within the last decade, and furnished within the last five.

The Thwaites' daughter Helen was not, in fairness, "pretty". She was a remarkably beautiful girl, tall and slender, golden-haired and blue-eyed in the best English tradition, with perfect skin and teeth and a clear, ringing voice. She greeted Crane with bright-eyed flirtatiousness, holding out both her hands to him. Crane smiled and disengaged himself, and bowed formally rather than taking Lady Thwaite's outstretched hand. Stephen lurked behind him, ignored.

The other guests were all in the drawing room.

"My dears," Lady Thwaite announced, "Our new earl, Lord Crane. Now, do you know everyone, my lord?"

"Nobody, I'm afraid," Crane said.

"Well, of course, you've spent so little time in Lychdale," Lady Thwaite said. "We're fortunate to have had as much of your company in this house as we have, when you're so busy. I'm sure I don't know what the attraction of our little home can be," she added roguishly.

"Oh, Mother," murmured Helen, dimpling.

Crane didn't smile at Lady Thwaite's sally, but moved forward to the other guests. The first was the vicar of Fulford, Mr. Haining, a fussy man in his fifties, quickly elbowed aside by Mr. and Mrs. Millway. This couple were obviously aiming to be part of the provincial gentry: a little too familiar, a little overdressed, and full of regret for the absence of the Thwaites' sadly delayed houseguests who should have arrived already, and who Crane would have found *so* charming. "*Dear* Sir Peter and *dearest* Lady B, you doubtless know them, Lord Crane?"

"I'm afraid not."

"Oh, but you must meet them! They live in London too!"

"What a remarkable coincidence." Crane turned to the last guests, the Vernons: a country solicitor and his plump, kindly looking wife, who regarded Crane with a slight frown.

"Pleased to meet you, Lord Crane," said Mr. Vernon, shaking hands. "I had a letter from your lawyers. About Allan Day."

"Good," Crane said. "I hope you found it informative."

"I did, yes. I was rather taken aback by it."

"You'd never have believed my father would do such a thing?"

"The letter didn't reflect well on him," Vernon responded carefully.

"Not much did."

Mr. Haining frowned. "Surely *de mortuis nil nisi bonum*, my lord?"

"Yes, and moreover, one shouldn't speak ill of the dead," added Mrs. Millway earnestly.

"Allan Day is dead too," said Mrs. Vernon, with an unexpected edge in her voice. "I thought it was an excellent letter, my lord."

"Who is this fellow?" demanded Lady Thwaite.

Crane stretched his lips in the shape of a smile. "A good man, grossly wronged by my father. On which note, let me introduce my guest. Mr. Stephen Day. Allan Day's son."

Everyone turned, looking slightly startled, as though they hadn't noticed Stephen till that point. Mrs. Vernon gasped aloud.

"Oh good heavens. Stephen Day? My goodness, it *is* you! How did I not see you there?" She flew over and grasped his hands. "Stephen! You used to play with our Richard, do you remember? He's in the army now. Oh, I'm so glad to see you well! But you're so thin!" Her eyes were filling with tears. "My dear boy. Come and tell me everything about yourself."

Wrapped in warmth and looking slightly stunned, Stephen allowed himself to be led to a sofa. Crane had to work to repress a smile and looked round to see Mr. Vernon wearing an identical expression to his own.

"He'll be lucky to escape Maria tonight," he remarked. "We always felt distressed that we lost touch with Day's family, when they left. It was a devil of a business. I'm glad the boy's well. Are you righting wrongs, Lord Crane?"

"Hardly. Let's say I'm tackling matters as they arise."

"You'll be here a while, then," said Vernon dryly.

Crane smiled at that. "Not if I can help it. I'm actually just here to deal with the legal matters around my inheritance."

"I thought I heard you were moving back to Piper?"

Crane shook his head. "If I stay in England, which is not certain, it will be in London. I'm not cut out for country life."

"Oh, but you must admit the country has some attractions," Lady Thwaite remarked from his side, and insinuated a hand onto his arm. With an effort, Crane didn't throw it off, but he did move his arm away, putting his hands behind his back.

"I dare say it has many attractions, but not for me," he said. "I like cities."

"Naturally." Lady Thwaite smiled. "But what if Lady Crane prefers a country home?"

"There is no Lady Crane."

"Ah, but some day, she may—"

"There is no Lady Crane, there is no Lady Crane in waiting, and I do not have any expectation of a Lady Crane *some day*," said Crane, biting the words out. "So the wishes of this hypothetical lady are hardly relevant."

Glances shot between the Millways. Mr. Haining stopped rocking on his heels for a second, and Helen Thwaite's lips pressed together, colour coming to her cheeks. Lady Thwaite gave a wide smile.

"Of course not, my lord," she said. "Single gentlemen never like to think of being caught in parson's mousetrap, as Sir James likes to call it." She gave a little laugh, in which some of the others joined, but Crane did not.

Her smile stretched, and she extended her hand invitingly. Crane kept his hands folded behind his back. Lady Thwaite's eyes flicked to his face. "My dear lord," she said clearly enough to be heard by others, holding out her hand commandingly. "Let us have a comfortable talk. Do give me your arm."

Crane had to fight to keep the revulsion off his face. The horror of the jack, and what had happened to Merrick, and Stephen's manipulation combined into a sickening whole, so that the idea of this bloody woman touching his skin—

And Stephen wasn't even paying attention. He was over the other side of the room, talking animatedly to Mrs. Vernon, his promise to defend Crane against fluence forgotten, and, perversely, it was a flare of hurt anger at that abandonment that made Crane extend his arm. He crooked it, but Lady Thwaite's fingers immediately found the bare skin of his hand.

She led him over to a sofa and sat with him, murmuring. "My dear lord, listen to me. You're here to see my daughter. She's very lovely, very charming. And you need to marry, don't you? You need to marry and you will choose Helen because she is lovely and willing and you need a wife..."

She muttered on in that vein. Crane contemplated her for a moment, then looked over at Stephen's back. Stephen casually lifted a hand to scratch his ear and his fingers gave a quick flutter in Crane's direction, like a tiny little wave, and a bubble of something intensely happy opened up in the middle of Crane's anger. Lady Thwaite was coming nowhere near his mind, because Stephen would not let her, and suddenly her murmured commands seemed not threatening but simply ludicrous.

He tolerated it a moment longer, till it seemed clear she was intent on nothing but a rich marriage for her daughter, politely disengaged his arm and rose. "Thank you, madam, that was most informative," he said courteously. "And I shall certainly take your views under advisement, although I fear you may be doomed to disappointment."

He left Lady Thwaite staring after him and went over to talk to Vernon again, as the only person present he didn't actively despise, until they were called in to dinner.

It was an intensely tedious evening. Lady Thwaite was coldly angry, and Helen's prettiness didn't conceal her building fury at Crane's failure to pay court. Sir James told a succession of hunting stories that were of no interest to anyone. The Millways were primarily concerned with establishing how many titled people they knew and trying to find mutual acquaintances with Crane, who lost all patience at the third reference to "your dear father".

"My father was no dearer to me than I to him," he said bluntly. "I couldn't tell you which of us was happier when I went to the other side of the world, but I assure you, I would not be within five thousand miles of here if he were still alive."

Mrs. Millway went pink with shock. "Oh, but he was your *father.*"

Mr. Haining nodded earnestly. "Surely there should be filial love—forgiveness—especially in a noble family—"

"No," said Crane.

Mrs. Millway opened her mouth and closed it again in the face of that uncompromising monosyllable. Helen Thwaite gave a tinkling laugh, with a slightly grating note to it. "Goodness me, my lord, you're terribly brusque. Is that how the best people speak in China?"

"If you mean the aristocracy, Miss Thwaite, I wouldn't know. I'm a trader."

"A tradesman. Dear me." Helen was bright-eyed and highly coloured, and her voice was vicious. "And what about your little friend? It's so interesting that you can't spare any time for courtesy to your neighbours but you've plenty of leisure for a *guest.* What exactly is Mr. Day doing for you?"

Her voice was loud. Heads turned involuntarily across the table, and Crane deduced from the various expressions of horror, embarrassment and excitement that his reputation had once again preceded him. Oddly enough, nobody looked at Stephen.

"Resolving some rather dull legal points about local issues," said Crane calmly, addressing Miss Thwaite as if unconscious of anyone else's interest. "Conveyances, I believe. Or possibly estouffements."

Vernon, the solicitor, coughed into his wine glass and loudly asked Mr. Haining about some parish argument. The Millways dragged in a not terribly relevant anecdote about a duke of their friend's acquaintance, the point of which was that the true mark of good breeding was courtesy and putting one's social inferiors at ease. Crane greeted this with a wolfish smile.

He didn't point out that nobody except the Vernons had made any effort to put the socially inferior Mr. Day at ease, because the little devil was obviously up to something. Crane could see him, and Mrs. Vernon, next to him, clearly could, but the rest of the company once again turned away as though he was literally not there.

Helen Thwaite continued to glower, made a few more unpleasant remarks, complained she had a headache, and left the table abruptly.

Eventually the meal ended. Crane sat through a single glass of port with the gentlemen before announcing that he would have to leave, after a private word with the vicar.

Mr. Haining was a thin, old-maidish sort of man, liver-lipped and almost completely bald, with a red birthmark disfiguring his scalp. Crane had taken his measure through the course of the meal, and wasn't disposed to be pleasant.

"Mr. Haining," he said without preamble. "Do you recall the case of Ruth Baker of Nethercote? Killed herself two years ago."

"A terrible business."

"I understand she's buried outside the Fulford churchyard."

"That's right. As a suicide...you understand."

137

"No, I don't. She was seduced by deception, at the age of fifteen, learned that she was carrying her own father's child, and killed herself. I'd have thought that a case for pity, not ostracism."

Mr. Haining's eyes bulged. "This is scarcely a suitable topic for a lady's parlour."

"There are no ladies here," Crane said. "Just you and me. What pastoral care did you offer this strayed lamb of your flock, Mr. Haining?"

"It's hardly my responsibility—" began the vicar.

"Actually, it is. Did you know her father, and seducer, was my brother?"

"I really feel that gossip is inappropriate—"

"How much influence did my father bring to bear on your decisions regarding the girl?"

"It was—that is—there were certain difficulties—the fact is— My position carries certain obligations to all levels of society, Lord Crane, and one must weigh—"

"Enough," Crane said contemptuously. "It is my opinion that Ruth Baker killed herself while the balance of her mind was disturbed. As such, she should be properly reinterred, in her local church. This ceremony should take place as soon as possible, at my expense. That's my opinion, and I think you'll find it's your opinion too."

"I'm afraid not, my lord," said Mr. Haining stiffly. "I must absolutely refuse to contemplate such a thing. It is a matter of the dignity of the Church. The great gift of human life is not to be thrown away."

He put up his weak chin. Crane let the silence stretch out to an uncomfortable length, until he saw the flicker of nerves in the man's eyes, then spoke very gently. "Vicar, I've let it be known that I don't propose to run my affairs with threats, intimidation or the abuse of power. That, in fact, I'm not like my brother or my father. I hope this has reached your ears."

The vicar looked at him hopefully. "Yes, it has, my lord."

Crane smiled and leaned closer. "The thing is," he murmured, "between us...I'm *quite* like them."

Chapter Fourteen

Stephen and Crane settled into the dogcart for the drive back to Piper. The wind was up now, and the night was at last suitably cold for April.

"What on earth did you do to the vicar?" Stephen asked. "He looked like he was going to cry."

"Sanctimonious prick. I told him that he'd rebury Ruth Baker within the week or there would be a new vicar in place within the fortnight."

"Can you dismiss a vicar?"

"If she's not properly interred by next Sunday, we'll find out."

They probably would at that, Stephen thought, looking at the set of Crane's mouth. "You seem very concerned by this."

"She was my brother's child. My niece," Crane said. "Which makes her baby—"

"Your brother's child."

"Yes, thank you. In any case, family. *Inoffensive* family. I think I have a responsibility there. And I do object to the stupid superstition of burial outside a churchyard. Might as well be at a crossroads with a stake through her heart. Talking of which, thank you for dealing with Lady Thwaite. What did you make of it?"

"Well, to be honest, I rather sympathised," Stephen said. "If that was my daughter, I'd be desperate to get her off my hands as well."

Crane snorted. "God, yes. What a foul-tempered girl."

"There's something really quite wrong with her, I think. She's angry about a lot more than not being Lady Crane. I wonder... Well, it doesn't matter. But I wouldn't marry her if I were you."

"You're full of useful advice tonight."

Stephen grinned. "Anyway, Lady Thwaite hasn't a hope of finding the girl a good marriage without fluence, and even then she'd be pushing her luck. So it's actually possible we don't have anything more complicated than that on our hands. I'll come back and speak to her formally tomorrow, then if I can get the haunting dealt with, I think that may be the end of it up here."

"Thank God. I loathe this place," Crane said. "Lady Thwaite, her idiot husband, that harridan her daughter, those dreadful toadies, and that grovelling hypocrite of a vicar."

"The Vernons are very pleasant."

"They are, but outweighed by the rest of the company. Not that you had to suffer most of the conversation. How did you do that?"

"What?" said Stephen innocently.

"You were hiding. I saw you."

"How could you see me if I was hiding?"

"I watched you. I didn't find it at all hard to concentrate on you, even if everyone else did."

"Oh. Well, I thought I'd rather not be noticed."

"You're good at that," Crane said. "You're a very unobtrusive, nondescript little man."

"Er—"

"Except for those eyes of yours," Crane went on musingly. "And those incredible hands. And that foxy smile. You don't let it out much, do you? Everything under cover. And then you stop hiding yourself for a moment, and your whole face lights up, and suddenly I can see just how you'll look when I fuck you."

Stephen's eyes widened in the dark. He knew he was blushing fiercely and felt distantly amazed he had any blood to spare from his groin.

"I came to a conclusion," Crane went on conversationally. "I want a great deal more of you and I intend to have it. I suggest we get away from this hole and start afresh. As it happens I own a hunting box in Northamptonshire—no live-in staff, simple, isolated. A few days a very long way from here, you show me what those hands can do, and I'll show you how we do things in Shanghai."

Stephen swallowed. "How is that?"

"Slowly," Crane said. "It's hot there. Very slowly, very thoroughly, inch by inch. You'll need a great deal of patience, or you might find yourself begging. I think you will, in fact. I'd like to hear you beg."

"Make me," said Stephen hoarsely, and grabbed for Crane as the other dropped the reins and reached for him. The taller man's mouth came down hard on his, long fingers in his hair pulling his head round, tongue flickering against his lips, perfectly shaven chin rubbing against his. Stephen brought his hand up to Crane's face, felt him jolt, realised he wasn't wearing his gloves, and jerked away, but Crane pulled him back.

He ran his hand down Stephen's chest and slipped a finger inside his shirt. Stephen gasped in Crane's mouth at the touch on his skin. Crane tweaked a nipple, hard. Stephen gave a little yelp and felt the other's mouth curve against his.

"Did you know," Crane murmured, "your hands fizz more when you're excited? That's going to be fun. No, keep them there. I want to feel this. I want to feel what you like." His hand was inside Stephen's waistband now, fingers playing and stroking. Stephen could feel he was leaking already, whimpered, an indistinct plea. "Oh, yes, you love that, don't you? Eager little thing. Jesus, your hands. I want them round my cock."

"It might sting a bit," Stephen muttered, but moved his hands down, then froze. "There's someone coming!"

"This bloody place." Crane released him and picked up the fallen reins again to encourage the semi-dozing horse back into a walk. Stephen jerked his jacket into place with trembling hands. He had the distinct sensation that his lips were bruised, and his cock throbbed painfully with frustration.

"We're not finished," Crane said softly. "And I want to feel those hands of yours all over my skin when I have you, feel what they do when I make you come. Christ, you're incredible."

"Shut up," Stephen hissed, as the approaching horse ambled into sight. It was ridden by a severely dressed man who doffed his hat as he went by, shooting a look at Stephen, who ducked his head, glancing away. Apparently completely unembarrassed, Crane gave a salute in greeting.

"That was the churchwarden," he said as the man passed. "I hope he finds Haining more use than I do. Where were we?"

"About to cause a public nuisance. This isn't safe, not out here."

"I suppose not," Crane said. "Will you come to bed with me?"

Stephen took a deep breath. "Not in Piper."

"Northamptonshire, then?"

"Yes. Or London." He looked at Crane, gave up the last shreds of control, and went on, "Or on the train down to London, or up against a wall in the nearest alley to the station, or anywhere else you like. Just not in Lychdale. Too many ghosts."

Crane paused, nodded. "Fair enough. First train to London tomorrow?"

"Lady Thwaite. Hector."

"Bugger them both."

"I'm not coming here twice. But...I could see Lady Thwaite early and get someone else to deal with Hector?"

"And we can get the midday train out of here. Right. Here's the turning."

The drained, deathly atmosphere of the house hit Stephen as they descended from the dogcart but Crane gave him no time to consider it. He swept Merrick up as he answered the door and bore them both into the drawing room.

"We deserve a drink," he said firmly, unstoppering the decanter. "The jack is dealt with, the Thwaite is thwarted—"

"Graham took the evening off," Merrick offered.

"And all's well with the world. Port or brandy, Stephen?"

"Don't touch the port, sir," said Merrick helpfully. "Graham waters it."

"Brandy, then. Thanks."

"I spoke to Haining," Crane told Merrick, returning to get a drink for himself. "He was—" He stopped, and gave a short, dry cough. "He was entirely—" He broke off again, coughed harder. "Blast this—" He made a hacking noise in his throat. Then another. His face convulsed and his hands came up to his neck.

"My lord?" said Merrick.

"Crane?" said Stephen.

Crane was gripping his throat with both hands, shaking his head, his skin suddenly white. He made an appalling retching sound and doubled over. His face distorted with horror, he gave an awful choking cough and opened his mouth, and Stephen saw that a mass of pale hair was bulging out up from his throat and between his teeth.

"*Christ.*" Merrick stared with disbelieving terror.

Stephen was up from his chair and over, skidding to his knees, grabbing Crane's head with both hands and pulling him to the floor. "Lock the door, Mr. Merrick," he said calmly. "Don't panic, Lucien. Breathe through your nose. Can you breathe through your nose?"

Crane sucked in a half-stifled breath through his nostrils. It whistled horribly. He made another dreadful retching choke and shook his head frantically under Stephen's rapidly moving, searching hands.

"Keep still. Try not to panic."

Crane heaved, and a matted double handful of hair spilled out of his mouth. His face was a dark, mottled colour now.

"Fucking do something!" said Merrick savagely.

"I...am." Stephen's hands were over Crane's skull, fingers wide and clawed, digging in. "In five, Lucien. Three, two, *one.*"

Crane convulsed, spine snapping back, tearing his head away from the painful grip. Stephen lunged after him and grabbed his shoulder. "It's over, it's over, let me get this out— stay still, I don't want to hurt your throat. Here." He started pulling the hair out of Crane's mouth, movements precise and gentle, as they knelt on the floor opposite one another and the shaking man sucked in deep desperate breaths through his nose. "Steady. It's all right, I've stopped it. Sit down. Mr. Merrick, he'll need a drink."

145

"Him and me both," said Merrick. "What the fuck was that? Sir."

"Attempted murder," said Stephen. "Keep still, Lucien. It's nearly over."

Crane kept still, as instructed, fighting the urge to vomit. He could still feel the dry scrape of hair inside his throat, and worse, though Stephen's prickling fingertips were only just inside Crane's open mouth, he could distinctly feel the sensation of gentle movements deep down inside his throat, scooping out the last of the hair. He closed his eyes and tried not to gag.

After a moment, whatever Stephen was doing in his throat melted away. "I think that's all."

Crane wiped the back of his hand across his face, began to speak, couldn't command his voice. He gulped from the glass Merrick handed him and tried again. "That was disgusting." The skin of his throat felt raw and scraped, and his voice was hoarse and shaking. "What the hell happened?"

Stephen poked the saliva-matted tangle of hair on the floor with distaste. His face was grim.

"Not to state the obvious, you've got an enemy," he said. "That was a calculated—hellfire!"

Crane looked at him in alarm that rapidly turned to paralysing terror as he felt the awful tangle of hair fill his throat again. He tried to call out but it was coming faster and harder this time, he could feel it thrusting and pulsing like some malevolent growth, blocking his airways, pushing down as well as up now. He opened his mouth to scream and felt the choking hair roll forward over his tongue.

Stephen seized his head again but almost immediately let go. The expression on his face was no longer one of calm professionalism. It was alive with rage.

"Candle," he snapped, holding out an imperative hand, taking hold of Crane's neck with his other hand as if to throttle him.

Merrick leapt to the side table, grabbed a candelabra and thrust it towards the magician. Stephen wrenched a lit candle out of it. He glanced down at the floor, up at the choking man whose throat he gripped. His pupils were so dilated that the tawny iris was all but invisible, leaving his eyes as black holes in his head.

"Don't move at all," he said, with stiff lips. "Choke—on—*this.*"

He turned the candle over. Crane had just time to register that the flame continued to burn straight and tall and *downward* before Stephen stabbed it savagely into the mass of wet hair on the floor in front of him.

Crane gave a desperate, shrieking gasp for breath, and inhaled again, more easily, as the hair in his throat shrivelled away to nothing. Stephen's left hand was gripping his neck firmly but not painfully. His right hand was white-knuckled on the candle. The flame burned downwards into the hair, licking out to all sides around the wax cylinder. The hair wasn't burning.

Merrick's eyes flicked to Crane's and down to the candle. Crane followed his gaze and saw that Stephen's nails were outlined with thin lines of red. As they watched, the blood seeped out and spread in a thin film across his nails and finger ends.

Stephen was frozen still, his whole body tense and concentrated. His eyes were black holes that looked at nothing, and the blood was gathering into drops on his nails. The air seemed shimmery, as though in a heat haze. Quite suddenly, all the candle flames in the room bent inwards at once, the flames streaming towards Stephen, and Crane felt the hairs on his arms and chest and head stir as if pulled in the same direction.

Blood drops were splashing onto the carpet from Stephen's fingers now, faster and faster, and Crane could feel a warm wetness on his own neck where Stephen's fingers dug in. He was arching backwards as though his spine was contracting, and there was a distinct red tinge to the light in the room that was starting to hurt Crane's eyes. The candles were all burning down at incredible speed, wax melting visibly. Crane saw Merrick's white-faced terror, realised that his own body was shaking violently, and belatedly knew that he was holding himself rigid to prevent himself from leaping up and running.

The mat of hair leapt into sudden bright flame. Stephen jerked forward, releasing Crane and dropping the candle, and the light snapped back to normality as Crane spasmed away from him.

Merrick stamped on the smouldering candle end, sat down abruptly on the floor and put his head between his legs. Crane wiped a shaking hand across his throat, and wasn't surprised to see the red stain on his hand or feel that his own skin was intact.

"Can you breathe clearly?" Stephen demanded, sitting back on his knees. "Anything at all happening now?"

Crane shook his head, lips clamped together. Stephen looked around the room, bloody hands stretched out to feel whatever strange currents he could pick up. He pulled a stained handkerchief out of his pocket with two delicate fingers, carefully wiped his nails, wiped the floor of any stray drops of

148

blood, returned the handkerchief to his pocket, folded his arms to stuff his hands under his armpits, and only then keeled forward, hissing, "Ow ow ow, blast it, *hellfire*."

"Are you all right?" said Crane. His throat didn't hurt as much as he'd feared.

"Fine. Fine. Stings a bit." Stephen did some deep breathing, in and out.

Crane got up on the second try, poured himself a very large brandy, spilling quite a lot, knocked it back in a single, painful gulp, sat on the floor again and began to swear. He swore fluently, inventively and with spectacular obscenity in Shanghainese until he ran out of epithets, switched to English, and started at the beginning again.

"You're feeling more yourself, then," said Merrick, when Crane reached an impressively foul climax.

"No, I am not. What the fuck, what the fucking, bloody devil-shit, what in the name of Satan's swollen cock was *that*?"

"Do you speak in the House of Lords with that mouth?" Stephen uncoiled his arms and shook his hands out. "Ouch. Can someone pass me the port please?"

"The brandy's better."

"The port's sweeter." He shook his head as Merrick started to pour him a glass. "Just the decanter please."

Merrick handed Stephen the cut-glass bottle, which he drank, gulp after gulp, from the neck, red liquid running down his chin. He downed the entire bottle's worth of port, took a very deep breath, and said, "Watered."

"You did that thing," Crane said. "Stripped yourself."

"Only a bit," Stephen said. "There's no *power* in this house." He wiped his hand across his mouth, replacing the trails of port with a smear of blood. "How do you feel?"

"Fine. Unhappy. You?"

"Angry." His voice rang with fury. "That was a vicious attack which was intended to be lethal. I will not tolerate it."

"What, exactly, just happened?"

"Someone got hold of some of your hair. They set up an equivalency, a...connection through the air, as it were, from the hair they hold, back to you. And they used the equivalency to multiply what they had, to create the hair that was choking you. I suppose you noticed it was identical to yours."

"Someone wanted to choke me to death on my own hair?"

"Someone wanted to kill you in a way that would be very hard to stop. It's a very old and powerful technique. The first attack would probably have killed you, but as it happens, I am good at equivalencies, so I broke it, and that should have been that. Except they set it up again in less than a minute, and they did it better and stronger and much harder the second time. And that's very bad."

"Why?"

"They have access to a lot of power," said Stephen. "They are strong. They were able to use a quite different technique. I couldn't even try to break the second channel as I did the first."

"But you did break it?"

"No, I used it. Sent the flame back up the other way. Burned the hair they held, for a start. I really need to eat something."

Merrick whisked out of the room. Crane put his clammy head in his hands. "What the hell is going on? Was that Lady Thwaite? Miss Bell?"

"If it was Miss Bell she is going to regret it very deeply, but not for very long. Or Aunt Annie— No. Lady Thwaite didn't seem to have anything to offer when I got in her way earlier, and there was real skill behind that attack, but it could have been her. Goodness knows you upset her. Did anyone pick hair off you that you noticed?"

"I honestly couldn't say."

"No matter. I can just find out whose house burned down."

Crane stared at him. "Are you serious?"

"Possibly. I did my level best to incinerate anyone at the other end of the channel. They were good but there will be evidence. Anything from scorched hair to a smouldering heap of wreckage."

Merrick hurried in with a plate of Mrs. Mitching's fruitcake. Stephen grimaced with resignation, but grabbed a thick slice and sank his teeth into it. After a few mouthfuls, he said, "You need to sleep. I am going to set up some wards round you, keep you safe. I'll keep watch—"

"You need to sleep more than I do," Crane pointed out.

"I'm going to. We are going to get through the night, and in the morning we are taking the first train back to London, where you are going to stay under the eyes of some friends of mine, while I come back here with a team of justiciars and tear this place apart. Mr. Merrick, I am going to need a lot of candles."

Chapter Fifteen

He set up the wards around Crane's bed. To the unskilled eye, it looked simply like a ring of lit candlesticks, until Stephen suddenly looked up from five minutes' intense concentration and all the flames simultaneously bent sideways, streaming out, as though in a circle of moving air.

"I'll sleep in the chair," he said.

"Your bed's in the next room." Crane was sitting up in bed, elbows on bent knees and head propped in hands, naked to the waist, magpies spread across his chest.

"There is *no power* in this house." Stephen tested the single armchair. It was predictably uncomfortable. "I want to be here."

"I'm glad you're here," Crane said. "Although when I planned for you to spend the night in my bedroom, this was not what I envisaged."

Stephen laughed, without much amusement. "This is definitely more what I'm used to. Try to sleep."

"I'm too scared to sleep," said Crane baldly. "I'm sorry to be a coward, but that was horrible. The thought it might happen again—"

"It won't," Stephen interrupted. "I've put up wards. They'll keep you safe."

"Candles. What do they do?"

"They'll keep off any etheric movement for a while. Not completely, not as long or as effectively as they would if I had access to power, which is why I'm staying here, but long enough that I'll be able to get to you before they break, if something starts."

"Get to me? You're six feet away," Crane said. "How long exactly—"

"*Enough.* I'm sorry, it's all I can do given I have nothing to work with, but it doesn't matter anyway. I'm here, and I'm not leaving you, and anyone who comes after you will have to get past me first. Yes?"

Crane gave him a long look that broke into a reluctant smile. "Thanks."

"Anyway, it's perfectly likely the perpetrator of tonight's attack is not going to be in a position to act," Stephen added. "With any luck, they're still on fire. I'm just being cautious."

"I approve," said Crane. "And tomorrow we run away?"

"Tactical retreat." Stephen shrugged off his jacket, and wrapped it back round his shoulders against the chill.

Crane twisted to lie on his side. "I suppose it would be distracting and unprofessional to suggest you join me over here?"

"Yes."

"It's going to be a bloody long night, then. Can I get up?"

"No. If you break those wards I'll choke you myself. They were hard enough to set up the first time."

"Because there's no power in this house. Isn't there some other way for you to get power?"

"Like what?"

"Magic wands. Magic rings. The Holy Grail."

"You have that here?"

"If I do, someone probably carved a magpie on it. Does it exist?"

"You wildly overestimate the extent of my knowledge," Stephen said. "As to magic wands and whatnot, there are...artefacts that act as focal points for etheric flow, but I don't have any to hand, and there's hardly any flow to focus." He frowned. "Unless—I don't suppose you have any of the Magpie Lord's things?"

"Such as?"

"I don't know. The ring in the picture?"

"Oh, probably," Crane said. "There's a pile of ancient jewellery in a room at the end of the Long Gallery, or at least there was. Do you want to go and look, at all?" he added, with a touch of amusement, as Stephen sat bolt upright.

"*Yes.* Yes, but tomorrow. Or I could— No. Stay in the wards. We'll look first thing tomorrow. If I find something to call on here, it'll be a different story altogether."

"And what if not?" said Crane.

"We run. As planned."

"Mmm. Could you strip someone?"

"What? No!"

"I meant with permission—"

"No," Stephen said again. "Sourcing from people is...it's the definition of a warlock. It's wrong."

"Surely in an emergency—?"

Stephen gestured for silence. "Look. You told me that you and Merrick were starving early on, in China. Really starving?"

"Yes."

"So hungry that you might have been prepared to do desperate things?"

Crane tipped his head back, contemplated the canopy of the four-poster. "So hungry that I did them. Your point?"

"Did you eat human flesh?"

"Did I *what*?"

"You can always find fresh meat in a graveyard," Stephen said. "And it's walking around everywhere you look, if you're prepared to butcher it yourself. All the meat you could want."

Crane opened his mouth, closed it again and held up an acknowledging hand. "Right. Fine. You've made your point."

"Exactly. Sourcing from people is wrong."

"Understood." Crane frowned. "No, wait. Warlocks are magical cannibals, yes?"

"That's a...vivid way of putting it."

"So if stripping people is as repugnant as eating them, how are there such numbers of warlocks as you've suggested?"

Stephen sighed. "Ah. Well." He curled his legs underneath himself. "The thing is, finding sources of power is the main preoccupation of most practitioners most of the time."

"For you?"

"No. No, I'm one of the lucky ones. I have—" He waved his hands vaguely. "I connect to the flow. I can pull power from the air, simple as breathing, where many of my peers would be gasping like asthmatics. It's easy for me. And I come to somewhere like Romney Marshes or here, and I realise what it must be like for the rank and file. Constantly gasping and grabbing and desperate. So you're ready to break the law to feed the need. It's hateful. I hate it. This house makes me feel sick."

Crane was watching him closely. "Are you all right?"

Stephen shook himself. "Sorry. I— It bothers me. I haven't exactly been at my best since I came here."

"I look forward to your best, then."

KJ Charles

Stephen gave him a tired smile. "You may even get it. Anyway, the point is...power is addicting. It's hard to drag it out of the ether, but it's so easy to tap people. Easy, effective, evil. And once one begins, terribly hard to stop, because the sensation of being without power is such a very horrible one. And of course it's tempting for any practitioner to see the unskilled as lesser—less talented, less able, less worthy of consideration—and if you tap them for power, you start to see them as lesser beings altogether. Cattle, they call them—you," he amended hastily. "There to feed on. There to use and discard. And that's a warlock, more or less."

"Cattle," Crane said.

"Yes. Sorry."

"Do you see the unskilled as lesser?"

"No," Stephen said. "I do a job that makes me hated by quite a large number of my peers, including many who aren't even warlocks, because I don't think anyone is entitled to exploit his fellows because of an accident of birth. You're an earl, I'm a practitioner, both of us were born this way, and neither of us is entitled to feed off other people because of it."

Crane considered that. "I'm bloody glad you're here."

"Really? Because I wish to God we were both somewhere else. Try and get some sleep, Lucien, it's late. And don't worry. I am watching you."

Stephen blinked, and realised it was morning. Golden light streamed through the gaps in the heavy brocade curtains. He was cold and damp and sweaty from sleeping in his suit, his neck and back ached from the cursedly uncomfortable chair, something was trying to attract his attention, and Crane was...

...right in front of him, shaking his shoulder.

"What happened to the wards?" Stephen demanded, jolting upwards.

"Nothing," said Crane. "They were still burning when I got out of bed thirty seconds ago. Listen."

Stephen's brain finally registered the sound that his ears had been trying to tell him about. "What the devil— Who's screaming?"

"I don't know. Merrick's down there finding out."

Crane started pulling on clothes as he spoke. Stephen hurried to his own room, rapidly changing into his usual clothing, and irritated that he found himself noticing the baggy knees and worn, permanently grubby cuffs. That triggered a thought, and as he jerked his boots on he called, "Wear something you can run in, please. No Savile Row."

"I don't get my suits made on Savile Row," said Crane, emerging in a casual grey tweed that still looked twenty times the price of anything Stephen had ever bought. "Wouldn't stoop to it. Come on."

They hurried down the stairs, ignoring Graham and a panicky-looking housemaid who had emerged. Other staff were heading outside for the source of the appalling noise. It was a dreadful sound, an endless, agonised shrieking in multiple voices, inhuman, and as they ran to the stables, they could hear a human voice too, a deep male sound, but sobbing like a child.

Stephen and Crane sprinted through the stable yard together and skidded simultaneously to a horrified halt.

Merrick was gripping the groom's arms. It was the coachman who had taken them from the station, but his usually surly face was distorted by grief and agony, and tears were running down his cheeks. Merrick was shouting at him but the words were inaudible above the noise the horses were making.

One lay dead in the yard, foam and blood still spilling from its open mouth, eyes and tongue bulging black out of its head. The others were all still alive, unfortunately. Eyes full of blood and fear rolled, swollen tongues protruded with dark sores that split open and spilled out a foul yellow pus, copious slime poured from distended nostrils. The horses thrashed and jerked in agony, voiding their bowels in terror, and the screaming went on and on.

Crane grabbed Stephen's shoulder and yelled over the hellish din, "What—the—devil?"

Stephen tried to reply, had to pull the taller man down to shout in his ear. "Get—rid—of—the—people."

Crane took a swift look round and saw that most of his staff were standing at the stable gate, frozen in horror. He sent them off with a few sharp words and returned to find Stephen shouting intently to the stableman.

"Equine plague," he was saying. "Got to be put down. I'm sorry."

The stableman turned pain-filled eyes on Crane. "They're in agony, my lord."

Crane put a hand on his shoulder. "Will you let me do it? Or let me help?"

The stableman's face twisted, but he looked at the five live horses and gave a brief nod.

Merrick had already gone. By the time the stableman had produced his rifle, the manservant was back from the house with two pistols.

They shot all five horses between them, Merrick, Crane and the stableman, and stood in the suddenly silent yard with the smell of cordite and gun cotton overlaying the stench of manure and blood, and the sound of gunshots and screaming still ringing in their ears.

"Go home, Varry," said Crane finally. "I'd drink myself unconscious if I were you, but do as you see fit. Take a couple of days. We'll find out more about this. I *will* find out, you have my word."

"Don't go near other horses for the moment," Stephen added. "There's a small chance of contagion."

Varry looked round at him in horror. "You think *I* gave this to them?"

"No, no, not at all. I meant it might have got on your clothes *from* them," Stephen said hastily. "It's just a precaution. But in fact, I think all the staff should go home, right now. They should stay away from horses and stay away from Piper for, oh, two days at least, starting as soon as possible. Mr. Merrick, can you get the house cleared in the next ten minutes, do you think?"

Merrick glanced at Crane, said, "Sir," and disappeared, pulling the devastated stableman with him.

"Why?" asked Crane.

Stephen turned on his heel and walked away from the stink of fear and death without speaking. Crane followed him, stride for stride, as Stephen marched out, over a stretch of unkempt lawn, ignoring the damp grass that quickly soaked his trouser legs, and up towards the lake.

"Why the horses?" said Stephen at last, as though Crane had only just spoken. "To stop us leaving. It's, what, twelve miles to the railway station? Three hours' walk. Plenty of time to catch us. Why make them suffer like that? To make us afraid.

159

Why clear the house? Because they're killers and they're probably coming here, and I don't want your servants in the way."

Crane was nodding impatiently, having worked most of this out for himself. "And who, exactly, are *they*?"

The sky was blue above, promising another hot day. The light was the clear gold that came just after dawn. The long grass was sparkling with dew, the tall trees surrounding the house looked fresh rather than heavy, the lake glittered blue and silver in the morning sun, its rippling surface brushed by whispering willows, and Crane would have given everything he owned to be back in the darkest slums of London.

There was a sudden flurry as a flock of magpies erupted out of the trees on their left. Crane jumped, and cursed.

Stephen took a deep breath. "I don't know who they are."

"Does this feel like Miss Bell?"

"Not at all. This was pure warlockry. Cruelty for its own sake, and to animals, and she's a hedge witch—a country practitioner. If she was behind that, I'll resign my commission right now."

"This is fucking ridiculous," Crane said. "I have literally no idea who is trying to kill me."

"I'm not sure anyone is."

"They were last night!"

"Yes, but they *didn't*," Stephen said. "There was no third attack. But they were able to strike this morning, and they struck at the horses, not you. Let me think." He pushed his hands through his hair, face alive with intense thought.

Crane kept pace with him, staring at the glittering lake, trying to persuade himself he couldn't smell gunsmoke and blood.

Then he stopped dead.

Stephen took a few more paces, and looked around. "Crane? What is it?"

"Stephen," said Crane thickly.

The practitioner was back at his side in two steps. "*What?*"

"I can't move."

Stephen's face froze. "Can't move at all? Try and take a step forward."

"I *can't*."

"Take a step back."

Crane took a step back and inhaled a deep, shuddering breath. "Christ. God."

"Did that hurt?"

"No. I just didn't think I could. What the devil..." He took a step forward, stopped in his tracks again. "What is this? I can't seem to move at all if I'm going this way."

Stephen's hands were twitching and sketching in the air, flitting round Crane's body. His mouth was set and grim.

"This is a binding. Someone has bound you within the limits of an area. Trapped you within your grounds."

"Well, can you deal with it please?" said Crane impatiently.

"I don't think so."

"What?"

"I don't have any idea how they did this." Stephen slid his hands through the air around Crane's shoulders. His pupils were wide and black. "I couldn't do this. I can't break it if I don't know what it is or how it works."

Crane took a deep breath, struggling for self-control. "Someone has poisoned my horses *and* trapped me in my own grounds?"

"Probably different people," Stephen said. "Why bother with the horses if you could do a binding like this?"

"Why are they doing this at all?"

"I don't know. I need to think."

"You need to do something about this!"

"I'm *trying*," Stephen snapped. "I'm sorry if I led you to believe I'm omnipotent, but I'm really not."

"That's becoming bloody obvious!" Crane snarled back, and swung away, getting himself under control. "Sorry," he added abruptly. "That wasn't fair. I'm—unnerved."

"I know. So am I."

Crane took a step back from the invisible barrier. There was a flutter of black and white as magpies landed around his feet.

"Bloody things." He made a cursory kicking movement to scare them off. They shuffled back a few inches, unafraid.

Stephen was watching with a frown. "They're surprisingly bold."

The trees were heavy with magpies, and a single bird was right in front of Crane on the path, glaring up at him with jet-bead eyes. "The place is infested," he said. "If you stand still, they gather like flies."

"They do, don't they," Stephen said slowly. "When you arrived. In the gallery. Have they always flocked to you like that? Even when you were a boy?"

"I don't really remember the behaviour of birds twenty years ago. Can we talk about the current problem?"

"Could you try to remember?"

"You want to talk about *magpies*? Now?"

"I'm starting to wonder if it's all about magpies," Stephen said. "Yes, now."

Crane gave him an incredulous look, decided not to argue, and shut his eyes in an effort of memory. "I don't know. The damn things used to flock round my father, all the time, but— that's right, never me or Hector. Because of course if any creature came near enough for him to throw a stone at it, he did. So they learned to avoid boys, I suppose. Father got fairly angry about it, he had a pet magpie and he couldn't understand why they flew away from us. I seem to remember it turned out to be my fault. There, does that explain everything?" he added, with some sarcasm.

"It's enlightening. Because your father was posthumous. Of course."

"What has that got to do with anything?"

Stephen pushed a hand through his hair. "Let me *think*."

Crane called on reserves of patience he rarely bothered to tap, and stood, watching Stephen's face as the younger man thought. It darkened and hardened as Crane watched.

Finally, Stephen looked up.

"I have a few questions," he said, in what Crane had come to think of as his professional voice, very calm and even. "First. Since your return, have you had intimate relations with anyone up here?"

"Have I bedded anyone, you mean? Not in Lychdale."

"Do you have any close living relations? Uncle, aunt, nephew, niece?"

"Only if Hector had other children. I'm not aware of any."

"Can you think of any means by which someone might have got hold of your blood in reasonable quantity? Any serious cuts or wounds? Teeth drawn?"

"No."

"Blood, bone and birdspit, and it's not blood or birdspit," said Stephen. "This is not good. Where's your brother buried?"

"The mausoleum," Crane said, not even bothering to comment on the non sequitur. "Round the other side of the grounds. Near the Rose Walk."

"And was it always this cold in Piper?"

"I can't say I remember it being so bad, no. I want you to explain this."

"I will," Stephen said. "But I don't want to start till I have time to finish, and we have to hurry. The servants should be out by now, shouldn't they?"

"With Merrick behind them, I expect so."

"Can you get rid of him too?"

"I doubt it," said Crane. "It's been twenty years and he's not left me in a sticky situation yet. Why do you want him gone? He may not be magic but I'd still back him against anyone I've yet met here."

"I'm sure," Stephen said. "But if someone threatened to do to Mr. Merrick what they just did to the horses, is there anything they couldn't make you do?"

Crane's face tightened. "Right. He's not going to take it well, though."

"I'll talk to him," Stephen said. "If we can get rid of everyone else, there will only be you and me to worry about."

"That was exactly why I wanted you to come to Northamptonshire," muttered Crane.

Stephen snorted, without much amusement, and led the way back. They trudged through the wet grass, dew flashing and sparkling in the sun, magpies fluttering around them.

Chapter Sixteen

The house had been emptied, except for Graham, who stood in the hall, having a raging argument with Merrick. Crane stalked over and spoke in low, cold, savage tones, his words making the old man go red and then white with outrage, until he turned and stormed out. Stephen was leaning against a panelled wall, eyes shut, breathing in a shallow, controlled way. It reminded Crane of his trance in the garden, a week ago, but then Stephen's face had been preternaturally calm. Now he looked tense, almost afraid.

At last the three of them were alone in the house.

"Right," Crane said to Merrick. "We're in an unspecified form of extreme trouble. I'm apparently being kept here by magical means that Mr. Day can't do anything about. I have no idea what's going on, he thinks he does, he's in charge."

"Thank you," Stephen said. "Mr. Merrick, there are at least three warlocks coming for Lord Crane, probably four. Bad shamans. What was that word?" he added to Crane.

"*Wugu.*"

"Shit," said Merrick.

"Indeed. I am outnumbered and, frankly, outmatched. I need you to go and get me some help."

Merrick scowled. "Where, sir?"

"London. Dr. Daniel Gold's surgery, Devonshire Street, off Oxford Street. You want Mrs. Esther Gold, but you can talk to Dr. Gold if need be. If neither of them is there, tell his people to get Mr. Janossi. I need Esther up here urgently, with Saint and Janossi. And tell her it's a sinkhole. Got it? Good. You're going to have to get to the station somehow. Steal a horse. Even better, go to Nethercote and tell Miss Bell that there's warlockry afoot, tell her to get you on the road to London. And listen, Mr. Merrick, don't trust anyone else. Not the vicar, not the stationmaster, not my aunt, not anyone. Don't let anyone touch you and try not to let them see you... I'm asking too much of you. This isn't safe."

Merrick's eyes narrowed. "What d'you reckon's going to happen, sir?"

"Someone may try to stop you. I don't know who. I don't know how hard they'll try. They might be prepared to kill. I realise this is a lot to ask but I'm afraid we're in a lot of trouble, and I don't have any other way out of it."

"What're you going to be doing while I'm gone?"

"Trying to keep Lord Crane alive," Stephen said. "My chances would be improved by reinforcements."

Merrick looked at Crane, who shrugged. "You heard him."

The manservant nodded briefly. "Right, then."

"Be lucky," said Crane. "And come back safe or I'll pursue you to the tenth court of hell to shout at you."

"You just watch your arse," Merrick retorted. "And nobody else's, *if* you can manage that. I'll get some stuff and be off. *Tse hue*. Sir," he added, with a nod to Stephen.

"*Tse hue*," said Crane.

The two gripped hands for a second. Merrick turned and ran lightly up the stairs. Crane looked after him, lips compressed.

"Was that Chinese for goodbye?" Stephen asked.

"See you again," Crane said. "Not goodbye. How much of that was true?"

"If I could have a wish granted, it would be to have Esther here right now. I have no idea if the enemy will be looking out for Mr. Merrick, but I'm absolutely sure his chances are a lot better away from you."

Crane took a deep breath. "Presumably, that's true of you too. I think you should go with him, Stephen."

"No. That ring, the Magpie Lord's, let's get it."

"No, we are going to talk about this. You didn't come here to get killed—don't just bloody brush me off," he added angrily as Stephen shook his head.

"It's pointless. They'll need to kill me anyway, don't you see? And we're wasting time."

Crane looked down at him. The shaman was quivering with tension, and Crane read a flat determination in his face. He turned on his heel and led the way upstairs, two steps at a time, feet echoing on the ancient stairs, ringing through the empty house. The shorter man hurried to keep up.

"This is guesswork, you understand," Stephen began. "And I'd be pleased to be wrong. Well. Do you recall when I arrived, almost the first thing I said was that this house reminded me of an Egyptian mummy?"

"Yes?"

"Does that ring any bells?"

Crane looked round at him as they strode towards the Long Gallery. "That chap in China. You last winter. Stripped people?"

167

"Spot on," said Stephen. "I think this house, this location is a very powerful source, and I think someone is stripping it. That means a human conduit is involved—they have to strip it *through* someone. And I can only think of one way that would work, and that's if Piper's power is linked to Piper's master. The Magpie Lord."

"He's been dead for centuries."

"Lord Crane is dead, long live Lord Crane. There's power in the Magpie Lord's bloodline. It's in the blood, bone and birdspit, as they say, and yes, birdspit is a euphemism. And someone is using your family to tap that power in a way which is extremely dangerous and utterly wrong and very, very effective."

"Using my family? They're all dead too."

"Yes. That's one reason it's wrong."

"I don't understand," Crane said. "I'm not magical, I'm not a shaman. Mine was absolutely not a magical family."

"Not actively, I'm sure, but look at the magpies." Stephen gestured at the paintings as they passed. "All you Vaudreys are reaching out to them, with your tapestries and tattoos, but they belong to Lord Crane, whoever he may be. They followed your father from birth because he was posthumous, he was born Lord Crane. They began to follow you once you had the title. The fact that they're still following you now is probably our only chance."

"How?"

Stephen made a little helpless gesture. "All the power is being stripped out of Piper and out of the Vaudreys, but the magpies are still with you. I'm hoping I can call on that. God knows there's nothing else for me to call on."

Crane threw open a door to a small study-like room and went to an old chest. "All the jewellery is in here," he said, opening it to reveal an assortment of boxes. "Now, tell me what the hell is going on."

Stephen knelt by the chest but paused before delving into it. Crane squatted down by him.

"This is going to be unpleasant." Stephen took a deep breath. "Right. Your brother impregnated his own daughter. Whether that was his idea or someone put her in his way...well, he did it. Someone told her, and she killed herself. So that's a Vaudrey girl with a Vaudrey baby in her belly, both dead, killed by her own hand, buried with shame." He pulled a box out at random and opened it to reveal a dull necklace of pale stones, which he stirred with a finger before discarding. "Ruth wasn't just a Vaudrey. She was a witch's granddaughter. And Gammer Parrott, of all the weapons she could have selected, chose a Judas jack for her revenge. Did someone help her to that decision? Help her to make the jack? I think probably yes. She had a good reputation all her life, and that wasn't a warlock's home. No, I think someone steered Gammer to make a Judas jack. And now we have your father and brother, two more Vaudreys, dead at their own hands."

He took out a couple more boxes, apparently at random, and opened them, blinking at tangles of dull gold chain.

"Perhaps the greatest source of power for a warlock is unused potential," he went on. "Life that goes unspent, growth that never happens. The strongest human sources of power are suicides—the murder of one's own potential—and unborn children, the closer to birth the better. 'Finger of birth-strangled babe', if you remember your Macbeth." He emptied another box unceremoniously onto the floor and ran his hands through the treasures without even looking. "In the last two years, we have three Vaudrey suicides, and an unborn Vaudrey child. I'm afraid I don't believe that's coincidence."

Crane tried to assimilate the litany of horrors. Stephen glanced up. "Do you recall what Hector's ghost was doing with his hands?"

"Trying to pull his head off, it looked like."

"I think he was trying to hold it on. Remember what happened when you hit him?"

"Vividly."

"I think someone has taken his head," Stephen said. "I don't believe his ghost just happened to start walking. I think someone took his skull and he wants it back."

He pulled out a couple more boxes. Crane was kneeling by the chest, totally still. He didn't think he could move.

"Are you all right?"

"No. This is the stuff of nightmares. You think someone has gone into my brother's tomb and cut the head off his corpse?"

"More than that," Stephen said. "You told the vicar of your intention to have Ruth Baker reburied. I'm going to guess that her body isn't in any coffin. That someone has taken it apart and used it, her bones and organs, her child, to strip Piper. That's probably why the vicar was unreceptive to the idea of her reburial, and actually, I bet it was he who tried to kill you. Nobody wanted you dead until then. But he couldn't let you discover her coffin was empty."

Crane gave up trying to sound calm. "You think Mr. Haining is a warlock? He's a vicar!"

"He didn't want Ruth dug up. And now I'm really guessing, but I think the reason there was no further attack last night, and the reason for trapping us here this morning, is that he, or his friends, learned I was a justiciar after the second attack. If they had killed you last night, I would have been straight over there, or straight down to London and back mob-handed. But if someone, maybe someone who had the word from Miss Bell, came and told them about me, their best bet would be to stop the attack and keep me here."

"Baines?" said Crane. "We passed him on the way back."

"*Who?*"

"Baines. The churchwarden—what is it?"

Stephen's face was working. "Baines. *Baines.* That's who he was! Oh, you stupid, self-indulgent *fool!*" He thumped a hand on the floor. "For God's sake, I thought he was familiar—but I didn't look at him properly—augh!"

"What is it? Who is he?"

"Hugh Baines," Stephen said. "He's a warlock."

"Dear God. How do you know?"

"Esther, my partner, had a run-in with him. It was a couple of years ago, and I didn't work on that job, but I should have recognised him—would have if I hadn't been too busy playing the fool, damn it!"

"Alright. You aren't perfect. Let it go. So your colleague didn't catch him?"

"He got away. Vanished, or at least we lost track of him. He must have come up here, I suppose. Miss Bell said there was a new churchwarden when Ruth was buried, didn't she? So Baines must have taken...the...position..." His voice trailed off. Very quietly, he said, "Oh God."

"What now?" The look on Stephen's face gave Crane a sense of sickening dread. "What is it?"

"Mrs. Millway was boring on about the Thwaites' guests from London who didn't come," Stephen said. "I didn't catch their names. Did you?"

"God, I don't know. She said it in an annoying way—Lady B, that was it. Sir Peter and Lady B."

"Bruton. Sir Peter and Lady Bruton," said Stephen dully, staring ahead despair in his voice. "Baines was Underhill's man. The Brutons are here. Of course. Of *course*. Underhill planned this whole thing. It's exactly his style."

"Who the hell's Underhill? Who *are* these people?"

Stephen didn't answer at once. He resumed his search, more urgently, emptying out an ancient leather bag which seemed to be full of loose stones and twisted bits of metal. "Right," he went on more calmly. "Here is what I think. A very dangerous man called Underhill set this up a long time ago, via, I imagine, Haining and Lady Thwaite, who knew about Piper, about Hector, about poor stupid Ruth. Underhill sent Baines up here as well, to get him away from Esther and help control things. I expect he was the one who got Gammer to make the jack, in fact. Haining refuses Ruth decent burial, Baines is full of sympathy... Easy enough to steer her, half mad with rage and grief. And Gammer died just as it was all coming together. Did she suspect something, I wonder? So that's Baines, Haining, Thwaite—the Brutons because they were thick as thieves with Underhill, and that makes five. And Underhill would have been the sixth himself, of course, but he's dead, so they've got a sixth warlock up here. I don't know who that is. Hardly matters, really. They could just be a makeweight with the Brutons and Baines in the group."

"Why must there be six?"

"You need six for a charnel posture," Stephen said heavily. "That's what the bodies are for. They're raping this house, and they're using your family's blood and bone to do it. A charnel posture. But that's a capital offence, so they have to kill me before I get to them. Hence the horses and the binding to keep you here, because that keeps *me* here, in a sinkhole. And since they'll have to kill me anyway, they might as well use you, alive or dead, because they can't risk me giving you any message for

Esther. And I can't do a damn thing about it because there's no power here!"

He flung away a bag with an excessively forceful gesture that betrayed his nerves and reached into the nearly empty crate for an ancient wooden box.

"If they're going to kill me anyway," said Crane, "and you can't stop them...why don't you go?"

"No."

"Stephen—"

"You know what happened to Mr. Merrick in China? Or the horses? They'd do worse to you if I left you alone. Not out of hate for you, nothing so clean, but purely so I'd always know that I saved myself at the price of leaving you to them. I've seen it before, Lucien. I'm not going."

"Yes." Crane felt his stomach churn at the thought. "I see."

"And if— *Oh.*"

"What?"

"Here." Stephen's hand delved into the jumble of ancient metal and picked out a ring, thick, dull old gold, carved. He held it between thumb and forefinger, face intent, and said again, "Oh."

"It looks like the one in the portrait. Is it?"

"I think it is. I think it's *his.*"

"Is it—useful?" *Please*, Crane thought. *Please.*

"Don't know," Stephen said. "I'd have to put it on."

"Well, go on."

Stephen glanced at him. "It's his."

"He's been dead for two hundred years!"

"I know."

Crane's breath hissed. "It's mine. He passed it down to me, just like the house and the land and the title. You have my permission to use it."

Stephen bit his lip. "I can't promise it will work."

"Just get *on*."

Stephen took a breath and slipped the ring onto his finger, gripped it with his other hand. He flexed his fingers, moved them. There was a short tense silence, then he shut his eyes, and Crane read the hope going out of his face.

"Anything?" he said, but wasn't surprised when Stephen shook his head without meeting his gaze.

"Sorry. It's got some kind of life, but... Well, maybe if there was some power here. But there isn't." He took a deep breath. "That's a blow. I was rather hoping..."

"It was worth a try," said Crane, not completely convincingly. "Is there anything else you can use?"

"Not here. I'm sorry." Stephen was staring at the floor. "I was staking everything on that, to be honest. Not that there's a lot to stake."

"Well... Hell. Let's find some weapons. No, leave that on."

Stephen paused in the act of pulling the ring off his finger. "It's not going to help."

"It's the Magpie Lord's ring, yes?"

"Yes..."

"Then wear it," Crane said. "In fact, keep it. It's yours."

"You can't do that."

"Of course I can. It was mine, I've given it to you."

"It's the Magpie Lord's ring!"

"And now it's yours." Crane held Stephen's gaze. "I might be his descendant, but you're the one doing his work. And..."

He reached out and closed Stephen's hand into a fist, his hand on top of the younger man's prickling fingers. "I think we could both use a little help with morale at this point."

"I... God. I don't know what to say."

"Say 'thank you, Lucien'."

"Thank you, Lucien," said Stephen faintly. "Well. I'll have to live through this just to show it off to Esther."

"That's the spirit."

Stephen contemplated the ring on his finger and looked up with a glow in his eyes that brought a smile to Crane's.

"Thank you, Lucien," he said again, his voice stronger, and Crane grabbed his shoulder and pulled him over for a hard, almost savage kiss. Stephen returned it fiercely, his hand tangling in Crane's hair and sending sparks running through his scalp. Tongues clashed, stubble scraped against stubble, and then Stephen's whole body stiffened with a rigidity that had nothing to do with pleasure.

"They're here," he said with utter certainty.

"Hell," said Crane. "Oh, hell."

Stephen stood. "Lucien, I'm sorry," he said. "I'm wildly outmatched. You've nowhere to run to. We will go and face them and I'll see what we can do but I will not make a deal with them. Not for my life or yours. If I do, they will own me, and I would rather be dead. If you choose to... Well, do what you must, but please, remember, to these people you're cattle. Just be aware."

"Understood. Is there any point in finding a weapon?"

"No. Let's just go."

They gripped hands for a second, silent, and strode together, feet ringing on the floorboards, through the Long Gallery and to the top of the Great Stair, and looked down to where a man and a woman waited. Crane heard Stephen's soft hiss.

"Oh, a morning call," said Crane, clearly and loudly. "How delightful." He glared down. The two strangers stared back, unmoved. They looked intensely solid, radiated something that was not quite a glow, a disturbing sense of immanent power. "And who are you?"

"Sir Peter Bruton and Lady Bruton." Stephen's voice was toneless. Crane glanced at him and saw his lips were white.

"Day," said Sir Peter. He was a tall, fleshy man, a little younger than Crane, large and physically powerful, with sunken blue eyes and a voice that drawled slightly. "I'm *so* glad it's you."

"I'm sure," said Stephen. "Did you miss me?"

"I won't miss you this time. I'm going to make you pay, you and the Jew bitch, and your whole band of self-righteous murderers, but I'll start with you, you vicious little pansy. You're going to scream before you die."

"Not as much as Underhill screamed," said Stephen venomously, and the air suddenly leapt between them as both men made violent motions. Crane jumped sideways as something he couldn't see distorted the world briefly. The big man made an abrupt flinging gesture, lunged with the other hand, and there was a heaving crack of soundless disturbance in the air. Stephen dropped like a rag doll, body crumpling as he fell, and tumbled down the stairs, limbs loose and flailing. He hit the floor hard, head smacking against the flagstones, and lay still.

Crane stared down at him, then met Sir Peter Bruton's eyes.

"You're in my house," he said. "Explain yourself, sir."

Chapter Seventeen

Crane sat in an armchair in the parlour with Lady Bruton opposite him. She was elegantly clothed in a green morning gown, very slender, with a pointed chin, large green eyes and soft brown hair fashionably dressed. She was the kind of woman who probably got called ethereal, Crane thought.

It would have been like any other morning call if he could stop wondering what Sir Peter was doing to Stephen's crumpled, helpless body, and if he had been able to move out of the chair.

Lady Bruton smiled at him. The sense of intensity came off her in waves.

"I'm so glad we can have this chat. I do want to see if we can find a happy solution. And I'm sure that horrid little man has told you all sorts of ghastly things about us."

"Not by name," Crane said. "He's mentioned warlocks."

"Warlock," she said, with gentle distaste. "Such a ridiculous word. There's no such thing, you know. There are just practitioners. Some of us choose to abide by a set of restrictive, outmoded laws. Some of us do not. And I'm afraid some people—nasty, small-minded, envious people—take pleasure in trying to bring everyone else down to their own petty level. A warlock, Lord Crane, is someone a justiciar doesn't like. They accuse us of murder under laws we don't accept, and they murder us and claim their law makes it right. It's very easy when you make the laws, isn't it?"

"Let me be sure I understand you," Crane said. "Do you use other people as sources of power? Strip them, use their corpses?"

"Well, of course we *use* people," said Lady Bruton, with a musical laugh. "We use the power granted to us as our birthright. Don't you, my lord earl?"

"I'm at best an accidental earl, and a highly reluctant one," Crane said. "And I believe I have your group to thank for my father's and brother's removal."

She smiled. "Perhaps you do. But tell me, what are you, if not an earl?"

"A trader."

"A trader. A good one? Successful?"

"Yes."

"Because of your natural talents," said Lady Bruton. "The fact that you are cleverer than the next man. Better at calculations. Luckier. More ruthless. Be honest: is not trading the art of exploiting those less gifted than yourself?"

"In part. It's better to ensure they'll trade with you again."

She waved that aside. "The fact is, we all of us have our place in life. Some of us are the nobility, some are the people. The people exist for the nobility. They are—"

"Cattle?"

"Yes. Cattle. The cattle that you farm for rents now, the cattle that you farmed for your trading. The mass of tedious, unimportant little lives, who are there to be of use to those of us who are above the herd. You and I know that is the truth, Lord Crane, I trust you won't pretend to be sentimental."

"What's sentimental is this claim to be justified by birthright. If you're going to murder people for your own benefit, you might as well be honest about it."

Lady Bruton's face hardened for a second, smoothed again. "You've been listening to Stephen Day," she said, with a note of lilting scorn. "You do understand it's motivated by sheer envy? All the justiciars are like that. They hate us because they want to be us: noble, unafraid, proud of what we are—proud of, yes, our birthright. They want to make us as cowardly and placeless as themselves. They're all contemptible: that common little queer Day, and his dreadful, graceless Jewess, and the rest." Her voice was no longer quite so musical. "Of course that plebeian runt has attached himself to you. You've birth, breeding, you're a fine figure of a man. Everything he isn't. It would be funny if it wasn't so revolting."

Crane settled back in his chair, feeling the invisible bonds hold him close. "What do you want with me, Lady Bruton?"

She gathered herself, gave him another dazzling smile. "I want you to make a choice. You see, we have a purpose here. We had hoped to pursue it without inconveniencing you, but Day *had* to get in the way. So now, I'm afraid you will have to serve our purpose, one way or the other."

"And the ways are—?"

"We'd like you to marry Helen Thwaite."

Crane blinked. "Miss Thwaite."

"Yes. She's a very pretty girl, isn't she? Perhaps a *little* difficult. Dear Muriel has struggled to find her a husband with her temperament, but that need not worry you. You need only give her, let us say, two sons, an heir and a spare, as they say, to ensure that the entail is fulfilled in the event of any mishap. We should hardly want your estate to descend to a distant cousin. But after that I dare say you could follow your own inclinations. Discreetly, of course. I should insist that you treat dear Muriel's daughter with respect, she is my very great friend, but—" She gave a little laugh. "I do understand men, you know."

"And how long would you anticipate I might live, once I've supplied you with the children you require to control my fortune?" enquired Crane.

"That depends very much on you, Lord Crane," said Lady Bruton gently. "If you make your fortune available to us willingly, that will be most welcome. And I need not scruple to tell you that we have ambitions to take our rightful place in the governance of this country. If you take your place in the Lords, in the seat of power, as our voice, you might make yourself quite invaluable."

"As your creature."

Lady Bruton smiled. "There's no need to be dramatic. After all, our servant will be everyone else's master. And there will be many compensations for your service, believe me."

Crane nodded. "And the alternative?"

She shook her head, smiling sadly. "You cannot leave this house except as our man, Lord Crane. Please understand that. Your death would serve our purpose really very nearly as well as your faithful life."

Crane looked at the lovely woman opposite him. Memories crowded in: Merrick's awful, imbecile rictus; the hair in his throat; the screams of the horses; the foul oiliness of the Judas jack. Stephen's crumpled body.

He was alone and entirely helpless, and he knew that there would be no mercy and no escape, and he didn't want to die.

He met her eyes. "I'm no stranger to compounding for my life, madam. Or to the awareness of death. I experienced, long ago, several months of degradation that I now find it astonishing I endured, but I welcomed it because the alternative was death. I know myself, my lady. I want to live."

"I'm delighted to hear you are so wise," said Lady Bruton warmly.

"So I can honestly say I would rather die than accept your offer."

There was a short silence. Lady Bruton's fixed smile suddenly had more teeth in it. "Really. And may I know the reason you choose not to join us?"

Crane took a deep breath, and told her.

Angry hands pushed hard, and Crane tumbled down the steps, unable to break his fall properly, landing heavily and painfully on the hard earth floor with his shoulder, a stone step gouging a long scrape into his arm as the shock jarred his brain. He took a harsh breath as the cellar door slammed shut, leaving him in darkness.

"Fuck."

"Crane?" said a disbelieving voice.

"*Stephen?* Christ. Stephen. Are you all right?"

"So far." Stephen sounded hoarse. "You?"

"Fine. Bruton roughed me up a bit. I annoyed his lady."

"How?"

"I told the whey-faced bitch what she and her repulsive cohorts could do with their offer of servitude. And then I stopped being polite."

Stephen chuckled weakly. "I knew there was a reason I liked you."

"You may be alone in that sentiment." Crane could still feel an echo of the shrieking agony that the enraged Lady Bruton had sent flaring through his bones. A bruise was swelling around his eye where Sir Peter had taken a more direct approach. "What happened to you?"

"Someone, presumably Bruton, gave me a reasonably savage beating. I made sure I was well out for it," Stephen said. "I woke up in here. He's cracked a couple of my ribs, I think."

Crane got himself awkwardly to his knees, hampered by the iron cuffs and chain that pinioned his hands behind his back. "Hold on." He moved over and tripped on a crate, falling to a knee. "Damn it. Can you make light?"

"I can't do anything. I work with my hands, and I've got iron round my wrists. I think Bruton might have stamped on my hands, actually. They hurt." Stephen's voice was controlled, but there was a tremor in it.

"Shit." Crane manoeuvred awkwardly until he bumped into Stephen's small, slight body.

"Sit back to back. Let me see if I can do anything about getting you loose."

"I'm in irons too," Crane said unnecessarily, feeling Stephen's fingers on his own, the other man's little sag of defeat. "Why can't you do iron?"

"It blocks the ether. You need to be strong as blazes to do anything with iron, and I'm very much not, right now." Stephen carefully let his body rest against Crane's, warm in the chill damp of the cellar, head heavy against Crane's shoulders. Their fingers met and held, tangling together, Crane very cautious in his movements as he felt the damp stickiness of the other man's hands, the flinching tension.

"What now?" said Crane eventually.

"We die, I expect. Sorry."

182

"Oh, well. I never thought I'd reach forty."

"You're very...calm."

"Well, I've been in a condemned cell before," Crane pointed out. "The novelty wears off."

Stephen actually laughed at that, a reluctant chuckle, and dropped his head back to rest against Crane's shoulder again. "That's aristocratic sang-froid, is it?"

"Certainly not," Crane said. "Just common or garden bloody-mindedness, much like your own." He gently stroked Stephen's raw, wet fingers, still adorned with the useless ring, feeling blood run down from the cut on his arm, not wanting to let go. "Tell me, why do that pair of lunatics hate you so much?"

"Thomas Underhill." Stephen sighed. "Third son of a duke. Very powerful, very influential, very clever. Bruton and he were old school chums, thick as thieves. Esther and I were after the pair of them for some time, but the world is full of idiots like Fairley who can't imagine a well-born warlock, and it was hard to pin them down. But eventually we caught Underhill red handed." He paused. "I do actually mean red handed. It was disgusting. Esther stayed to put the victims out of their misery, and I went after Underhill. I caught up with him on Romney Marshes."

"Ah."

"Esther came after me but she managed to break her ankle stepping in a rabbit hole, and when they found me I was half dead, and by the time she was able to identify Underhill's workshop, it had been dismantled. By Bruton, I have no doubt. We made our accusations public, Bruton denied them, but our word is good, so Bruton and his lady are being seen for what they are now. They left London precipitately, two months ago. Esther and I were going to go after them when I recovered." He took a long breath. "So, I killed his friend and I've made him known as a warlock. Bruton is not going to spare me. And he won't spare you either."

"What are they likely to do, any idea?"

"I imagine they're going to use you as a live conduit for the power of Piper. That would add enormously to the effect of what they're doing. I'm surprised they offered you an alternative, to be honest."

"It wasn't an attractive alternative. Stephen, can you strip me?"

"Lucien—"

"I mean it. I don't want to be a live conduit. I'd rather be a dead nuisance. I'd rather die at your hands than theirs. And I'd rather give you a fighting chance. If you do it—"

"I know," Stephen said rawly. "I know. Don't. I can—try and kill you. If you like."

"I would very much prefer you to live. I think those maniacs have plans that need scotching. Lady Bruton talked about their rightful place in ruling the country. She wanted me to speak in the Lords for them."

"Did she, by God." Stephen's hand twitched against Crane's. The drying blood felt tacky, bonding their fingers lightly together. "I don't know, Lucien. I don't know if I could do it, I've got iron on my wrists. And even if I could, I don't know if I *can*."

Crane started to object, stopped himself, and let the breath out on a long hiss. "Oh, the devil. I don't know. Use your judgement, God knows that's your role in life. I put myself in your hands when this whole ridiculous mess began, and I don't regret that so...do as you think best." He paused. "I just wish I'd had you in my bed, that's all."

Stephen's fingers tightened on his, and Crane felt the quiver of pain. "So do I. I'd have liked more time with you."

"A lot more time. Stephen, you're the only spark of light I've encountered in this whole vile country. You're extraordinary. You're valuable. And I don't want you to die because of me."

"Lucien..." Stephen took a very deep breath, fingers grasping Crane's hard. He gave a little gasp. "Lucien!"

"Listen."

Footsteps, approaching, up at the top of the stairs. The door swung open, sending light spilling down the stairs, making Crane blink. He felt Stephen's hands tighten convulsively on his own, as if grabbing for something that wasn't there. Then Bruton and Baines marched down the stairs, and Bruton's fists closed on Crane's jacket, dragging him up, and Stephen's hands were torn from his grasp.

Chapter Eighteen

They were marched, blinking, into the garden, near the Rose Walk. The sky was blue and cloudless, the enclosing greenery lush, the scent of roses almost unbearably sweet. Magpies chattered and screeched in the surrounding trees, but none came close.

There was a thing on the old stone pedestal. Crane squinted at it, unable to make it out, the shape making no sense, a mass of brown and yellow and clay colours and angular forms. As they approached, it began to resolve itself into something recognisable, and Crane said, "*Jesus Christ.*"

"He won't help you now." Baines shoved Stephen down, onto his knees. He gave a yelp of pain as he hit the ground. Forewarned, Crane was already bending at the knee as he was forced down next to the smaller man, so that he kept his balance, even with his eyes locked on the thing on the pedestal.

"Stephen. What the fuck is that?"

"The charnel posture," said Stephen in a thin, painful voice. "I can see Ruth Baker. Your brother's head. The baby."

"But they're posed like they're—"

"I know," said Stephen. "The degradation of the bodies makes it easier to tap the power, they say. Actually, I think they just like to do it."

Mr. Haining, standing behind the pedestal, fixed him with a malevolent look and opened his mouth, but Lady Thwaite elbowed him sharply. His bald head was reddened with burns and he had no eyebrows left. He glared resentfully at Stephen. Next to him, Helen Thwaite was staring sulkily at Crane.

"Miss Thwaite's a warlock," Crane observed, almost beyond surprise.

"Oh, I don't think so," said Stephen dismissively. "No— she's a flit. The runt of the litter. Virtually powerless. Just about enough talent to know what she's missing. It won't work, you know," he told Lady Thwaite.

"Of course it will." She and Helen were both looking at Stephen with loathing.

"It really won't. She'll get a taste of true power while you run the charnel posture but it won't unlock her potential, if that's what it's supposed to do, because she hasn't got any. It'll just drive her mad because for the rest of her life she'll fully understand what she'll never have."

"Don't listen, Muriel," said Lady Bruton.

"She'll be in the bedlam within three years, if she's still breathing," Stephen went on. "She's here to make up the numbers, nothing more, and the taste of power it gives her will destroy her. If they told you otherwise, they lied."

"Make him be quiet," Lady Bruton snapped, and Baines lashed out, catching Stephen on his temple, knocking him sideways. He gave a cry of pain.

"Heroic," Crane told Baines contemptuously. "Old women, idiot children, bound men, you'll take on all comers. There's a three-legged stray dog hangs around the lanes here. Perhaps some day you could work up to kicking that."

Bruton walked over and backhanded him across the mouth, his ring splitting Crane's lip open. "Shut up. Everyone, in position."

Crane licked the blood off his lip, breathing deeply, and sat back on his heels as the six warlocks spaced themselves in a circle round the foul display. He and Stephen were surrounded, bound, helpless, and even he could feel a subliminal throb in the air, a sense of brooding, intensifying power. The six looked alive, vivid, as if more real than everything around them. Haining's burns already appeared less angry, and Helen Thwaite's wonderful hair glowed, so lovely to look on it almost hurt.

Bruton began to murmur. The obscene mess of death on the pedestal seemed to quiver, to move, and Crane looked at it with horror.

"They're drawing down the power," said Stephen softly.

Crane turned and looked at him properly for the first time. Stephen's face was swelling, one eye half closed, blood dried around his nose. He looked pale and shaky and sick, and very intent.

The warlocks shuffled forward, closing their circle round the filthy tangle of bones and skin. Bruton took out a long knife and tested the edge, turned slowly and looked over at the two kneeling men with relish.

Hell and the devil, thought Crane. After all he'd seen and done, everywhere he'd been, this was the end, at last, and it had to be here, in bloody Piper. "Stephen..."

"Who are you going to kill first?" Stephen asked, with not quite enough bravado.

Sir Peter and Lady Bruton glanced at one another.

"Kill Crane," said Helen pettishly. "He's horrid."

Baines gave her a look of contemptuous dislike. "We kill the justiciar first. Get rid of him now."

"I want to make the pansy watch," said Lady Bruton.

"Which one?" asked Haining with a smirk, and there was a ripple of laughter.

"Day." She was talking to her husband. "Kill Crane and make Day watch. I want you to see his face when his boy friend screams for help, when he knows he's failed before he dies. For you, and for Thomas."

Bruton swept her hand to his mouth and kissed it. "My dear. Perfect."

"*Lucien*," said Stephen, and as Crane turned, he lunged awkwardly sideways, intent unmistakeable, and Crane met his mouth with his own. Their lips hit painfully, and Crane moved to cover Stephen's mouth in one last, desperate kiss, and felt the other man's teeth sink viciously into his torn lip.

It was excruciatingly painful. He jolted, but Stephen was pulling as he bit, and sucking hard, dragging Crane's bloody lip into his mouth, and chewing on it, even as Bruton's fist hit the side of his head, so Crane's flesh tore again as they lurched apart.

"Degenerates," said Bruton with disgust. He grabbed Crane's arm, hauled him to his feet. "I'm glad you're dying today."

Crane looked round, bewildered, betrayed, mouth aflame with pain. Stephen was hunched over, head down, shoulders rounded, a small, defeated heap.

Bruton pushed Crane forward a step towards the obscene altar and the knife.

"Wait." Stephen was still staring at the ground. "Stop. Please. Just...one moment. One."

189

Bruton turned, face twisted with contempt. "Go on, Day. Beg."

"One," the little man whispered. "One…"

"One *what?*"

Stephen looked up. His lips were red with Crane's blood, and his eyes were wide black pits ringed with molten gold.

"One for sorrow," he said, and there was a soft clink as the iron at Crane's wrists fell away and hit the grass by his feet.

Stephen blinked, and a flutter of black and white danced across his eyes.

"Two for joy." He spread his chainless arms wide, and something that wasn't there, something black and white with a flash of metallic blue, seemed to unfurl beneath them.

"Peter!" screamed Lady Bruton.

"Day!" roared Bruton.

"Five thousand for justice," said Stephen, and the magpies of Piper rose off the trees around them in one huge, terrible, boiling cloud of black and white and glittering blue that blotted out the sun.

Then the birds descended.

Bruton bellowed something and grabbed Crane's arm. He felt a sudden awful suction, like the way the candles had bent towards Stephen but in his own body, and the instant realisation that Bruton was trying to strip him was matched by an equally instant physical reflex as he spun, snapped his skull forward and broke Bruton's nose with a crunch.

It was a dogfight after that. Crane didn't try to see what was going on, in the swirling mass of beaks and claws and feathers, the clouds of dust that the wingbeats raised from the dry ground, the endless, awful screaming. He didn't look to Stephen. He simply tried to keep Bruton busy.

Aside from his powers, the man was close to Crane's height and much bulkier, a little younger, much less tired. He had every advantage except one: he fought like a gentleman, not a Shanghai dock rat.

Crane went for eyes, ears and testicles, using teeth and nails and knees. The magpies screamed and clawed and stabbed around them, and Crane hit and twisted and ripped, and the two men rolled on the ground together, Bruton desperately trying to fend off Crane's vicious assault, Crane equally desperate to keep the man occupied, until, with a grunt of effort, Bruton gathered the shreds of his strength and an invisible force pushed Crane violently away and flung him onto his back on the earth, knocking the breath out of him. Magpies rose away from the ground in a cloud.

Bruton roared something incoherent through bloody lips, rising, pulling his hand back to strike, and there was a sharp, loud retort that echoed off the stonework around them. Bruton jolted, a stunned expression on his face, and fell forward. Crane looked down at the shattered bloody mess of his skull, and up at Merrick, standing a few yards away, holding a smoking pistol.

"I thought I told you to go to London," Crane said.

"Yeah, well."

There was a hoarse shriek from the other side of the Rose Walk. Merrick turned and sprinted and, instinctively, Crane followed. They both vaulted benches and dodged through thorny growth, and skidded to a halt, seeing Miss Bell, features distorted with effort, both hands out, as if trying to push away the scratched, bloody form of Lady Thwaite.

"Oi!" bellowed Merrick.

Lady Thwaite looked round and gave a cry of fury. She pushed hard at Miss Bell, who staggered back, her face twisting.

"Put down the gun! I'll kill her!" Lady Thwaite crooked her hands in a clawing gesture, threatening, but there were tears running down her cheeks.

"Step away from her," said Crane. His mouth was agony as he spoke. "You've already lost."

Lady Thwaite turned on him with a tear-stained face full of hate, and stopped abruptly.

"One chance." Stephen's voice came from behind Crane. "No mercy. Down or die."

Lady Thwaite's eyes darted from side to side. She looked again at Stephen, gave one suppressed sob, and made a sudden lunge towards Crane, which stopped almost instantly. She shook for a second, a gout of blood erupted from her mouth, and she fell forward.

There was no question in anyone's mind but that she was dead before she hit the ground.

"What the hell was that?" said Merrick.

"Judgement," said Stephen.

He walked forward, five feet tall, and Crane knew that even the most lethal killers of his past would have shrunk back to let this man go by at this moment. His eyes were their normal tawny colour again, but every time he blinked, a flutter of black and white and blue danced across them. Magpies pecked and jumped around him, and gathered silently in the bushes and trees around them. There was a heavy thump as one landed for a moment on Crane's shoulder.

Stephen looked intensely solid, almost vibrating with energy. His face was dirty and spattered with drying blood, but he didn't look beaten, and his fingers weren't raw and crooked, and he no longer moved like a man in pain.

He glanced down at the woman he had just killed, and up again.

"Miss Bell. And Mr. Merrick. What, exactly, are you doing here?"

Merrick shrugged defensively. Crane tried to remember the last time his henchman had felt the need to justify himself. "Went up to Miss Bell's place, we had a little chat, reckoned we might do more good here than on a train. So we come over. Got here about five minutes before they brought you out. Miss Bell had her eye on the brown-haired lady, and I had a gun on the big sod the whole time. I was just about to take the shot when—" He made a gesture with his hands, fingers fluttering upwards and outwards. "Didn't realise you had it under control, sir, beg your pardon."

"In fact, I didn't. Thank you." Stephen nodded acknowledgement, and something in the atmosphere relaxed slightly.

"You, on the other hand," Merrick went on to his master, "you need to get your hands dirty more. Letting that bloke kick you off."

"Did not. Swine used magic." Crane spat blood onto the ground.

"So *you* say."

"I refuse to get involved in this," Stephen said. "And Miss Bell? Why are you here?"

Miss Bell looked slightly self-conscious. "It's like what you said, before. There's no good doing the right thing unless you stop people doing the wrong thing. Is there?"

Stephen smiled at her, the real, crooked smile that lit his eyes. "There isn't, no. Thank you, Miss Bell. Thank you very much."

She huffed. "I didn't do anything, in the end."

"You held that cow off," said Merrick supportively.

"You came to help," said Stephen. "You *acted*. I appreciate it."

He walked forward, holding out his hand. Miss Bell stepped around Lady Thwaite's body, took it, and immediately snatched her hand away again with a sharp intake of breath. "What the— how are you *doing* that? Why aren't you burning up?"

"Good question. Come on." Stephen started back to the other side of the Rose Walk.

Crane took a long stride to catch up, and Stephen turned to him. "How's your mouth?"

"Hurts."

"I am sorry, Lucien. I didn't have any choice. Here." He reached up, and as his fingers closed round Crane's jaw, the prickling turned to a warm, intense glow that rapidly grew searing. Crane made a noise of protest, but Stephen held on with a soothing murmur for a few seconds more. "Better?"

Crane explored his lip with a cautious tongue, realised that his bruised eye was also eased. "Yes. Much. You can heal wounds?"

"Me? No. This is borrowed. From Piper. The charnel posture's broken, the flow is coming back." Stephen gave him a swift smile. "There's power in this house."

"So I see. Tell me, if, as I deduce, the ring is giving you access to the Magpie Lord's power, why exactly did you leave it quite so bloody late to use it?"

"It wasn't on purpose," Stephen said. "I worked it out in the cellar. Your blood had met mine, on our hands, and when I tried to do—something—I felt the power stir, and I realised. Stupid of me. It should have been obvious that the ring needed Vaudrey blood. But there wasn't enough from just our hands, and I was about to say so when those swine came in. And then I had to find a way to get more of your blood into me before they killed one of us. That got a bit closer to the line than I'd have liked."

"Yes, it did, didn't it," said Crane, with some restraint. "So it came down to blood, bone and birdspit in the end?"

"Indeed."

"Does that mean, if you'd just come to bed last night—"

"Probably." Stephen pushed through the roses. "Shut up."

"I didn't say a word," said Crane, grinning.

They were back in the open space by the Rose Walk, and Crane looked around for the first time. The ground was covered with dust and feathers and uprooted grass, bare earth now at points. Bruton lay on his face, blood wet on his shattered skull. Haining was on his back, blood trickling from his mouth and nose, eyes dark and bulging, not breathing. Beyond him was a vaguely human form that Crane glanced at once and turned from.

"Who was that?" he asked.

"Baines," said Stephen. "The magpies had him."

Crane's eyes flicked again to the bloody, sprawled mess on the ground. White ribs showed through the torn skin and flesh. "Why?"

"He made the charnel posture, I think. They didn't like that."

"The— Where is it?" demanded Crane, belatedly realising. "The damned thing's gone!"

"The magpies took the remains. They'll have burial under the sky. I think probably the birds know what's best for Vaudreys, in Piper." Stephen was looking at Miss Bell, not Crane. She nodded abruptly.

Crane was frowning. "Haining, Baines, Bruton." He strode over to the stone pedestal, looked behind it, flinched at what he saw.

"Stephen, you should see this."

"I felt it." Stephen didn't move. "Lady Bruton stripped Miss Thwaite, yes?"

"Someone did." Crane couldn't take his gaze off the terrible rictus of staring eyes and clenched teeth on Helen Thwaite's yellow corpse. "And Lady Bruton's nowhere to be seen."

Stephen sighed. "Lady Bruton clearly persuaded her dear Muriel into this business with the promise that Helen could be turned into more than a flit by the power of the charnel posture. She was virtually talentless and knew it, and it was driving her mad. Easy enough to dangle a cure in front of her mother."

"Would it have worked?"

"No idea. Maybe."

"And Lady Bruton stripped Helen to get away. Lady Thwaite chose to die just now, didn't she?"

"She was going to anyway," Stephen said. "Don't feel too sorry for her. She chose her path."

"Maybe, but the other lady was the worst of a bad lot, if you ask me." Miss Bell gave an emphatic sniff.

"Inarguably," said Stephen. "And I will catch up with her, in due course."

"I'm sure you will." Crane looked around. "Meanwhile, what do we do with all the bodies? And what the hell do we tell Sir James?"

"We'll have to burn the Thwaites, at least. Is there any chance of a tragic house fire?" Stephen asked Miss Bell.

Miss Bell tapped her lip thoughtfully. "Baines's house would do. It's isolated enough."

"But what would Lady Thwaite have been doing there?" asked Crane.

Stephen shook his head. "It doesn't matter. Look at the corpses, Lucien, we can't let people see that. We fire a house with the bodies in it and leave a terrible mystery, or we burn them here and their families never find out they're dead. I say the former unless anyone has a good reason not to. Let's leave Bruton and Haining here, I'll get the magpies to take them. And I hope someone drove, because we're going to need a carriage."

Chapter Nineteen

Later—significantly later, leaving an isolated house burning—Stephen Day finished washing his hands in the scullery and walked back through Piper's long corridors until he reached the library door, outside which Crane was leaning, propped by his shoulders against the doorframe.

"Hello."

"Hello," Crane said. "How are you feeling?"

"Fine. More or less. How are you?"

Crane's eyes narrowed. "Are we having a polite conversation?"

"It's been a fairly trying day," Stephen said. "If you need some time for reflection—"

Crane reached out, jerked him off his feet, pulled him into the library, and shoved him against the door to push it shut.

"Right," he said, leaning down into Stephen, voice low and intent. "There is now plenty of power in this house. You're perfectly capable of throwing me across the room with a thought. Right?"

"Yes...am I going to want to?"

"Let's find out," said Crane. "Because the hell with ghosts, the hell with families, I intend to have you, right now, and that's not up for discussion or reflection."

He wrenched Stephen's shirt off as he spoke, jerking at the buttons, dragging the torn, filthy linen over his narrow shoulders.

Stephen's mind stuttered to a stop. In the brief respite since he'd finished killing people and burning bodies, he'd veered between the fear that the end of the danger would spell the end of Crane's interest, and the fantasy, sternly pushed away, of a private compartment on the train home with uninterrupted time for Crane's perceptive, teasing lovemaking. He had not expected to be unceremoniously fucked against Piper's walls with the blood barely washed off his hands.

Not here, he thought helplessly, as the old fear of this house, this family stabbed through him again. Not like this.

Crane's hands stroked Stephen's thin bare chest, lined white with faded scars, brushed his nipples and slid down to his hips, where Stephen's body, unlike his mind, felt no doubt at all. The long fingers ran over his stiff cock, his arse, then flicked the buttons at his waist open, and Stephen made a stifled noise that was somewhere between need, protest and terror.

Crane pulled sharply back to look into the shorter man's face. His hands were still firm on Stephen's body, his breathing ragged with lust, but his eyes were questioning, concerned, and with that second's pause, Stephen could think again.

Hector was long gone. Piper was cleansed, purified by fire as the bodies burned and the fresh air rushed in. The hands that claimed his body now had held his bloody fingers in the darkness of the cellar.

The past was dead. They were alive. He wanted this man so much.

Right here, right now, *exactly* like this.

"*Yes,*" he said aloud, and saw the smile in Crane's eyes for a second before the man hauled him up and into a ferocious kiss.

As soon as they broke for breath, Stephen grabbed for Crane's belt, hands sparking and prickling. They kicked and wrenched each other's clothes off impatiently, and Stephen gave an astonished gasp as he saw the final two magpies that adorned Crane's body, one across a lean hip and the top of his groin, one on the opposite inner thigh.

Crane gave him no time for admiration, let alone second thoughts. He'd long concluded that Stephen thought a great deal too much. Instead he picked the smaller man up, clear off the ground and pushed him against the wall, holding him up with one hand as the other probed with practised skill. Stephen, whimpering, wrapped his legs round Crane's hips and grabbed on to his shoulders, and the power in his hands spangled through Crane's skin like shards of diamond, leaping with Stephen's gasp as Crane's fingers worked inside him, opening him, tormenting him, and their cocks jutted hard against each other's bodies.

"Oh God," Stephen whispered. "Please. Please, Lucien…"

Crane ran his tongue up Stephen's neck, nipped his ear. "Tell me what you want. Exactly what you want. Let me give you the fucking you deserve."

Stephen took a shallow breath and looked into Crane's eyes, direct and naked. "Take me. Right now. Make me beg."

Oh sweet God. Crane was well aware that Stephen's tastes ran in harmony with his own, but that surrender was still a jolt right to the groin. "At your pleasure," he said thickly, lifted the him away from the wall and half-fell with him onto the desk where Stephen had lain on his back just the day before. "Hell. I need—"

Stephen's hand was on Crane's cock, and there was a sudden sensation of slick wetness. "Done."

"Slippery little witch." Crane pushed into Stephen's body, spread before him for the taking. Stephen's hands clawed his back, their touch like a burn that intensified as he drove harder, deeper. He pressed on Stephen's shoulders, holding him down, using words and cock and fingers to bring him to the edge of ecstasy, and Stephen writhed and thrashed and cried out with breathless pleas as Crane mastered him with deliberate roughness, spurred by the fizzing, sparking hands that betrayed Stephen's pleasures and demanded more.

Crane took him thoroughly, almost brutally, and when he had fucked him into helpless, whimpering submission, he pulled back and almost out, and lifted Stephen's hips, before plunging in at an angle of attack that had the little man gasping.

"Please. Please. Oh God, I can't—"

"You'll take my cock whenever I want to give it to you." Crane lifted him clear off the desk as he thrust into him. "Won't you?"

"Yes, my lord," Stephen whispered.

Crane gritted his teeth against his own climax at those breathy words and all they implied, feeling Stephen's hands flare with ecstasy like burning rain on his skin. "Say that again. Beg me to fuck you."

"Oh God, don't make me—"

"Say it." Crane drove in as hard and deep as he could.

Stephen cried out, desperately. "Please, my lord, please fuck me, my lord, fuck me, *fuck me*—"

It turned into a scream as he bucked violently, and as Crane felt the hot wetness spurt against his belly, Stephen's hands tightened convulsively on his hips with a surge of power that sent Crane suddenly, uncontrollably over the edge of his own climax, spilling into Stephen's body, howling as he fell.

Crane let Stephen flop back onto the desk and slumped over him. Their rasping, gasping breath mingled for a moment of silence.

"God," Crane said finally. "For a quiet man, you fuck like a mink."

Stephen didn't respond to that. He was completely still for long enough to make Crane wonder if he was regretting their act. Then he gave a sudden, convulsive shudder, and his whole body spasmed into rigidity.

"Stephen?"

Crane pushed himself up on his arms, withdrawing as gently as he could. Stephen didn't react. His eyes were wide and blank.

"Stephen!"

His pupils enlarged terrifyingly, blotting out the gold irises, and returned to normal equally quickly. He blinked and focused on Crane's face.

"Lucien."

"What is it?" said Crane sharply. "What's wrong?"

"Nothing. Nothing. I—" He broke off, staring at Crane's chest.

Bewildered, unnerved, Crane looked down too and saw...

"The hell. What the *hell*?"

His tattoos were moving. The birds hopped and turned and stretched, fluttering over his skin, two-dimensional but alive.

Stephen laughed out loud, a stunningly joyous sound. He pressed his hand against Crane's chest and gave a whoop of glee as a magpie flurried along his fingers, up his arm, and began to explore his own chest with its inky beak.

"It took me years to get those done," said Crane, more or less at random. "I'll want it back. Oh my God, look at the woodwork!"

Stephen tipped his head back. The magpies carved on a line of decorative panelling were moving, pecking and shifting. One took off along the length of the frieze in a flurry of wooden wings.

"I bet the entire house is doing this," Stephen said, face alight. "I want to see your Great-Aunt Lucie's china set. And the tapestry!"

At that Crane started to laugh too, watching incredulously as the magpies fluttered around them. Two of his tattoos were now hopping across Stephen's narrow chest, pecking at an old burn scar. "What's going on? Why is this happening?"

"I think we're the Magpie Lord," Stephen said. "Me and you. You in me. Your blood and my power and the ring, together. This is how Piper wants to be, can't you feel it? It's warm again. It's alive." He looked alive too, and much younger without the constant air of nervous tension that had dogged him for so long. He was happy and vivid, and glowing with pleasure, and Crane stared at him, unable to imagine how he had ever seen this man as drab and unmemorable.

"You amaze me," he said. "Continually and wonderfully. Is this going to happen every time we fuck?"

"Only when it's as good as that." Stephen's lopsided grin was particularly foxy. "Honestly, I've no idea. We could find out empirically."

"Which means...?"

"Do it a lot more and see what happens."

Crane pulled him upwards, wrapping the small lithe body in his arms. He felt Stephen nestle in to him with a satisfied purr, and kissed the top of his cropped head.

"Ready when you are," he said.

About the Author

KJ Charles is an editor by day and a writer by night, living and working in London.

KJ blogs about writing, editing and life on both sides of the publishing fence at kjcharleswriter.wordpress.com, and tweets as kj_charles.

Magic in the blood. Danger in the streets.

A Case of Possession
© 2014 KJ Charles

A Charm of Magpies, Book 2

Lord Crane has never had a lover quite as elusive as Stephen Day. True, Stephen's job as justiciar requires secrecy, but the magician's disappearing act bothers Crane more than it should. When a blackmailer threatens to expose their illicit relationship, Crane knows a smart man would hop the first ship bound for China. But something unexpectedly stops him. His heart.

Stephen has problems of his own. As he investigates a plague of giant rats sweeping London, his sudden increase in power, boosted by his blood-and-sex bond with Crane, is rousing suspicion that he's turned warlock. With all eyes watching him, the threat of exposure grows. Stephen could lose his friends, his job and his liberty over his relationship with Crane. He's not sure if he can take that risk much longer. And Crane isn't sure if he can ask him to.

The rats are closing in, and something has to give...

Warning: Contains m/m sex (on desks), blackmail, dark pasts, a domineering earl, a magician on the edge, vampire ghosts (possibly), and the giant rats of Sumatra.

Available now in ebook from Samhain Publishing.

It's all about the story...

Romance

HORROR

www.samhainpublishing.com

CPSIA information can be obtained at www.ICGtesting.com
Printed in the USA
LVOW11s1745011014

406763LV00006B/697/P